IN THE ENDS

Also by Alex Wheatle:

Liccle Bit

Crongton Knights

Straight Outta Crongton

Home Girl

HODDER CHILDREN'S BOOKS

First published in Great Britain in 2023 by Hodder & Stoughton

1 3 5 7 9 10 8 6 4 2

Text copyright © Alex Wheatle, 2023
Cover illustration copyright © Berat Pekmezci, 2023

The moral right of the author has been asserted.

*All characters and events in this publication, other than those clearly
in the public domain, are fictitious and any resemblance to
real persons, living or dead, is purely coincidental.*

All rights reserved.
No part of this publication may be reproduced, stored in a retrieval system,
or transmitted, in any form or by any means, without the prior permission
in writing of the publisher, nor be otherwise circulated in any form of binding
or cover other than that in which it is published and without a similar condition
including this condition being imposed on the subsequent purchaser.

A CIP catalogue record for this book
is available from the British Library.

ISBN 978 1 444 96963 4

Typeset in Palatino by Avon DataSet Ltd, Alcester, Warwickshire

Printed and bound in Great Britain by Clays Ltd, Elcograf S.p.A.

The paper and board used in this book
are made from wood from responsible sources.

Hodder Children's Books
An imprint of
Hachette Children's Group
Part of Hodder & Stoughton Limited
Carmelite House
50 Victoria Embankment
London EC4Y 0DZ

An Hachette UK Company
www.hachette.co.uk
www.hachettechildrens.co.uk

I'd like to dedicate this book to all the consultants and staff of Luton & Dunstable University Hospital who cared for me, and still do, since I had taken ill in early 2023. Save the NHS and may they all receive a generous pay packet!

My name is Jonah Hani, and I live on the second floor of Priestley House in South Crongton. My life is kinda stressed right now since my pops got booted out of his job. My parents have been flinging insults at each other like grime artists having a beef.

I don't wanna get tangled up in the kitchen or the front-room war zone, so I spend most of my time in my room.

My parents moved to the UK in 2001. They wanted to live in London but were offered a flat in South Crongton.

Pops worked for several years at the housing department in Crongton Town Hall. Stress licked his forehead every other day. Mum worked part-time shifts in a bakery near Crongton Broadway. Our stomachs were well blessed. She'd come home with Victoria sponges, apple pies, rum, raisin and carrot cakes.

Life was sweet.

I always owned the latest mobile-phone upgrades, any trainers that tickled my fancy, and I got my hair trimmed at Raymond's Neat Clips barber salon whenever I wanted.

Then, Pops got made redundant. Money worries was all my parents talked about in the evening. In the middle of the night, my seventeen-year-old sister, Heather, had to intervene to kill their screaming and hollering.

I'd normally be taken out for a restaurant treat on my birthday. Not any more. Mum forever told me to switch off lights I wasn't using. Shopping trips to buy name-brand garms in Crongton Broadway were a thing of the past.

In recent months, my friends and I had our own dramas.

We got caught up in the North Crong–South Crong war. We just about escaped by the skin of a school-dinner gravy.

You can't help but bump into gang lords and their followers in and around our estate. In North Crongton you have Major Worries. Some peeps say that if you stare at him for too long, he'll carve your throat with a hard look. Here in the dirty south, peeps still whisper about Manjaro. He hasn't been seen for the longest time. The feds are hunting him and peeps who live in the ends hush their voices when they say his name.

In the far north of Notre Dame reigns G-Gore. His kingdom is branded the Land of Never. Never cos any outsider who steps into that cursed land never returns.

My friends and I call ourselves the Crongton Knights. I can't remember who came up with the name. It might have been McKay cos he's always loved up castles, body armour, long swords, chopped heads and shit.

There has not been so many gangland shankings in recent weeks. Things have gone quiet. We've felt more at ease stepping around South Crong. We haven't ventured on any kinda mission outside the ends.

But the murmurs persist. North Crong graffiti is sprayed on South Crong slabs. South Crong Gs go missing. Nobody dares to step to the north side of Crongton Park. Young South Crong peeps make sure they don't stay too long after dark on Crongton Broadway.

McKay, one of my best friends, is fretting about his older brother, Nesta, who is always getting himself in trouble.

The last thing I want in my life is a perilous new mission. But it's coming . . .

1

Food Bank

My calf muscles proper ached when I reached my gates. A lion that had suffered an asthma attack couldn't have had its chest heave more than mine. My track coach, Mr Smallwood, had gone all SAS survival course on me. I just wanted to dip in the bath, listen to some grime and sink into my sleep zone.

As soon as I opened my front door, I heard them. Miss Crow, the ancient half-deaf widow who lived on the ground floor, probably caught my parents' tones too.

Well embarrassing.

'Gabriel!' my mum shouted at my pops. 'Gazing at your feet isn't going to pay the rent! We're broke. Are you going to go down to the food bank or not?'

I stepped quietly along the hallway and reached the kitchen. I stood under the doorframe. The plain black-and-white clock tick-tocked above my head. My heart kicked into third gear, as Mr Smallwood would call it.

Dad was parked at the table. He held his forehead with his left palm and stared at the floor. Mum stood over him with her arms crossed. Her eyes laser-holed into Dad's cheeks. She hadn't noticed that I had arrived home.

'Don't tell me I went to see the doctor for nothing,' Mum went on. 'I told her about my high blood pressure and our money issues. She gave me a prescription and a voucher for the food bank. Don't expect me, with all that I've got on, to go down to Crongton Broadway.'

'I wouldn't expect you to walk to the Broadway and carry stuff home from there,' Dad replied.

'Are you going to use the voucher?' Mum wanted to know.

Dad lifted his head. He wiped sweat off his cheek. He spotted me. He tried to raise a smile, but stress smacked it down. 'Jonah,' he greeted me. 'How your running go today?'

I had joined the athletic club at school. Mr Smallwood said that if I worked hard, I had the skills to compete at the highest level.

'Hard,' I replied. 'Mr Smallwood had us running through the wilderness up in Crongton Heath. Trust me, there are some strange flies up in those ends. Smallwood said it'll build up my stamina.'

Mum turned round and looked at me. 'Did you shower after your running?' she asked.

'Er, no,' I replied. 'Gonna soak in the bath now.'

'Take a quick shower,' Mum insisted. 'You'll use less water. Even hot water is expensive these days.'

She turned her attention back to Dad, who looked at his raggedy brown slippers and shook his head.

I made my way to my room and flopped on to my bed. I closed my eyes. I knew my parents were about to boot off for the second half. There was always a second half. I could hear everything cos the walls and doors were skinny in my house.

'How are we going to manage?' Mum started up again. 'At the end of the month we must find money for gas, electric and everything else. And you've been out of work for what . . . ?'

'Seven months,' said Dad. 'I've been trying. You know I've been trying.'

'Not hard enough,' Mum snapped. 'I don't know why you won't take a job riding those little motorbikes delivering pizzas.'

'Because it's humiliating,' Dad cut in. 'I used to work in an office at the town hall. I had a good position.'

'If you don't do something soon,' Mum yelled, 'the next position you'll be in is under a bridge in a sleeping bag!'

'It won't get as bad as that,' said Dad.

I soft-toed back into the kitchen. I wanted a glass of water.

Mum gave Dad one of her brutal eye passes as I turned on the cold tap. 'Are you going to pick up the voucher and go to the food bank?' she asked. 'If not, you can take that damn pride of yours, pack it in a suitcase and get out!'

Silence.

Did I just hear that? Mum just told Dad to get out!

I filled my glass and made my way back to my room. I sank half of it and crashed on my bed again. I picked up my pillow and covered the back of my head with it in case they went into extra time. My heartbeat shot into fourth gear. For a moment I imagined Dad sitting near the entrance of a supermarket with a skinny, smelly dog begging people for loose change. My forehead felt as if you could sizzle a strip of bacon on it. *Can fifteen-year-olds suffer from stress or heart attacks? I wish I had the funds to pay off our debts.*

Usually when my parents booted off, I'd play a game on my Nintendo and slap my headphones on. But I was too tired to reach up to my shelf for them.

I opened my eyes.

Looking down at me from a poster was Usain Bolt in sprint pose wearing the yellow, green and black of Jamaica.

One day maybe I'll be styling South African or British colours as I step into my blocks for the Olympic final of the four hundred metres. Yes, that's a dream and a half. If it did happen, Mum and Dad could scope me from opposite ends of the stadium. I don't want them warring when I'm burning around the track.

There was a knock on my door.

Food Bank

I didn't know why my family bothered, cos they never wait for an answer. They just bounce in.

Sure enough, Dad stepped in. He carried his head so low I could see his bald patch – I'd never noticed it before he lost his job. He shuffled forward half a stride. Suddenly he looked older. 'When you've showered you can follow me to the food bank. I'm going to need some help carrying the stuff home.'

'But I'm seriously tired, Dad,' I said. 'Have you seen those hills on Crongton Heath? Well-fit mountain goats and Sherpas would have untold trouble climbing those peaks.'

'If you can run up hills for Mr Smallwood,' Dad replied, 'then you can follow your old man to the food bank.'

He lowered his head, turned around and left my room.

I hoped no one at school would see me in the food bank zone. I grabbed my biggest hoodie and pulled it over my eyebrows. *If I had a Black Panther mask, I'd wear that.*

I glanced at Usain Bolt. *Bet you didn't have to fret about any food bank mission.*

As Dad and I left our flat, I spotted Liccle Bit bouncing up the steps of our slab. I had told him after school that I'd be home about seven. It was quarter to eight.

'Thought I'd drop down and play a couple of games with you,' Bit said. 'Where are you going with your pops?'

I waited until Dad stepped down two flights of stairs before I replied. 'Doing a bit of shopping,' I lied.

'Shopping?' Bit repeated. 'I thought your mum and

your sis do all the shopping in your yard? About time you take a turn. I've been stepping to the supermarket for the longest time.'

'Mum's not feeling too good and Heather's out at some save-the-youth-club-building meeting.'

'Jonah!' Dad bellowed from below. 'I haven't got all night!'

'Gotta move,' I said.

'See you in the morning,' said Bit. 'And say a big hello to Heather.'

I caught up with Dad and we trekked to Crongton Broadway. He didn't say a single word on the trod. Off the Broadway was a side road where the poshos worked out at the Crongton Fitness Suite – they had this purple lighting in the windows. Next door, they ate skinny pizzas and fat garlic bread at Luigi's Bologna Bar. There was Hatty Daniels' coffee shop too which sold little butterfly cakes and caramel shortbread for more than three notes. Mum said they were a con job. The food bank was at the end of the road. *I'm glad it's not the High Street cos I'd be bound to be scoped there by someone I know.*

'Follow me in,' said Dad at the entrance.

I hesitated for half a second, but I did what I was told.

The aisles were narrow, but the shelves climbed high. There were no discount stickers, buy-two-get-one-free deals or any promotional displays. I had never seen so much tinned food. Carrots, beans, chopped tomatoes, pilchards, corn beef, spaghetti, tuna, ravioli, Spam, butter beans, tinned custard, fruit cocktails and more tuna.

There were untold boxes of digestive biscuits but none of them were chocolate.

Dad reached the counter and presented his voucher to a red-haired woman with long green fingernails and a gold stud in her nose. 'Thank you,' she said with a half-smile. 'Happy to help.'

Dad didn't say anything. He sort of grinned back. He collected a trolley and started to fill it with cereal, margarine and eggs. Cornflakes packets outnumbered every other cereal about ten to one. I couldn't spot any Sugar Puffs, Frosties or Coco Pops. *Damn*.

I had never felt proper poor before but now I did.

As Pops wondered what to fling in the trolley, I kept my radar on the entrance, hoping I wouldn't recognise anyone – especially a fit girl from my school. That would've been tragic.

We were inside the food bank for no more than ten minutes, but it felt like hours.

Dad gave me two plastic bags to carry home. It seemed as if I was lifting the whole North Sea catch of pilchards in one of them. Smallwood would've been well proud of me.

I stepped outside and nearly crashed into Morgan Stapleton riding a scooter. *Oh shit!* He was in my English and history classes. He had a weird-shaped Afro and frying-pan ears, but kids nicknamed him Sky because he spread news and gossip. He couldn't help himself.

Deep-cave explorers considered taking on Morgan's mouth as their next expedition. He looked me up and down as if I had a dinosaur growing out of my left nostril.

'Jonah!' he said. 'What you ... What you ... Did you go running with the track team today?'

'Yeah,' I replied. 'Smallwood took us up to the wilderness.'

'Crongton Heath?' wondered Morgan.

'Yeah,' I replied.

He studied my bags as if they had a hot picture of a *Love Island* chick on them.

'Smallwood's real dream is to train army commandos,' Morgan said. 'That's why I didn't join the track team. If you don't mash it up at the regional championships, he'll probably go all horror movie on you.'

'Yeah,' I said. 'I can't lie. He can be intense.'

'Playing ball in the park is enough for me,' Morgan said. 'Anyway, later will be greater.'

He glanced at my food bank bags one more time before he rolled away. I hoped I wouldn't see him at school tomorrow.

'Jonah!' my dad called. 'Stop loafing. Let's get this food home.'

I wanted to step back to my ends the backstreet way, but Dad wasn't feeling that. I pulled my hoodie over my eyes. I could hardly see where I trod.

When we reached home, we dumped the food in the kitchen. Mum inspected it as if she were a forensic fed at a murder scene. She put on her glasses to read the sell-by date.

'No cooking oil?' Mum asked. 'Didn't I tell you to get some cooking oil? You expect me to fry your eggs with my own saliva?'

I left the kitchen as my parents started round three.

I spotted Heather's jacket hanging in the hallway. I knuckled her bedroom door.

'Who is it?' she asked.

'Jonah.'

Silence.

'Oh, all right,' she finally said. 'Come in, but I'm not in the mood for any of your whiny sulks.'

I entered. Heather sat in front of her dressing table mirror delicately taking off her eyelash extensions. It looked painful. My maths teacher, Mr Gorham, would've liked the neat curve of my sis's Afro. I could've used it as a protractor. She was wearing her fave Black Lives Matter T-shirt.

'Why do you wear those spidery things on your eyes?' I asked. 'You sure you can see in them? And I *don't* sulk.'

'None of your business why I wear my extensions and yes you do sulk. Big time!'

She put on a squeaky voice and imitated me. 'I can't get an upgrade or the new iPhone!'

I sat down on Heather's bed. I sniffed whatever perfume she was wearing. Rihanna stared down above her dressing table. Heather's uni books filled a shelf and her cuddly-toy tiger cubs watched me from a corner. I'd had plenty of dreams where the cubs grew into man-eaters and munched Heather alive. I half-grinned.

'What you smiling at?' Heather wanted to know.

'Oh, nothing.'

'Hmmm.'

'Do . . . do you think they will break up?' I asked. 'Mum was saying to Dad that if he doesn't get a job quick-time he can get out.'

Heather thought about it. She stared into her mirror. She then turned around to look at me. 'Three or four months ago I would've said no. But now . . .'

She shook her head.

'What's gonna happen?' I asked. 'You think . . . you think Dad will have to step? He's sad times three these days.'

'Close the door,' she ordered.

I kicked the door shut.

'Mum's under serious stress,' Heather explained. 'Sometimes she says things she doesn't mean. It's just her wages we're living on. She only does twenty hours a week at the bakery. They get housing benefit, but I don't know how much.'

'So why are we in rent arrears if we're getting housing benefit?' I asked.

'It's complicated,' Heather replied. 'Dad having to go back to South Africa to bury Grandma didn't help. Don't know how much that cost or if he took out a loan. He won't tell me.'

'I wanted to go.'

'Me too,' said Heather. 'But you can't have everything. Everyone's gonna have to sacrifice something. I might have to look for a part-time job myself to help out.'

'Where?' I asked.

'I dunno,' Heather replied. 'Maybe in a bar or a coffee shop.'

'Get a job at the Cheesecake Lounge so me and my bredrens can get freeness,' I laughed.

'Hmmm.'

I'd seen my sis with her study lamp on in the bird-snore hours of the morning. She revised when we were sinking dinner. Heather didn't have any time for a part-time job unless the day increased to thirty hours. I finally realised how serious our situation was.

'So, Jonah,' she said. 'I don't want you bitching in my ear corners about the latest iPhone upgrade or what brands you wanna style. For now, you're gonna have to dump any luxury dreams to the back of your head.'

'I don't bitch,' I argued.

Heather gave me one harsh side-eye. 'Yes, you do! Times three.'

'No, I don't!'

'I haven't got time for this debate, Jonah. I've got revising to do so you're gonna have to step. Stress and worries might be going on in my yard, but I can't let it affect my uni work.'

I stood up and walked towards the door.

In The Ends

'Oh, one more thing,' said Heather. 'I heard a rumour on the road that Manjaro's back on the kerbs.'

'Manjaro!' I repeated. My shadow flinched. The heat in my forehead blazed like the after-burners of a moon rocket.

Some time back, Manjaro had manipulated Liccle Bit into hiding a gun. That had caused all kinds of nail-munching drama. Me and my bredrens didn't wanna go back to that page again.

'Jeez and creeps!' I raised my voice. 'How? Where? Did someone scope him? What are the road men saying?'

'It's just a rumour,' Heather said. 'I think . . .'

'You think?' I asked. 'What do you mean, you think? You know he tried to delete Liccle Bit and his grandma, right? You know he's a proper South Crong jackal? Man on kerb say he's killed three North Crong youts. The feds have been hunting him for the longest time. FBI probably want to jail his behind too.'

'Jonah, you don't have to tell me about Manjaro. I went to school with him. Remember? He was in Year 11 when I started at South Crong High. His name came up in a meeting we had about the youth club. Apparently, he used to play table tennis there.'

'What did someone say?' I wanted to know.

'That he was seen in a backseat of a car,' Heather replied. 'Stop fretting! People claim to see Manjaro every day. It's nothing new.'

'I'll have to tell Liccle Bit.'

'Don't go freaking him out,' warned Heather.

'You just scared the ribs outta me,' I said. 'You didn't care too much about that!'

'*Don't* tell Lemar sugar-nothing,' Heather insisted. 'His family have stressed out enough over that South Crong G.'

'But he's my best bredren,' I said. 'I have to clang the alarm. Some peeps on the road think Manjaro's dead. Liccle Bit thinks he's safe.'

'He *is* safe,' replied Heather. 'Manjaro won't terrorise him. If he wanted to, he would've come back a long time ago. Remember, Manjaro has a baby with Liccle Bit's sis.'

'But I have to say—'

'No, you don't have to say,' Heather cut me off. 'Say *nothing*. I mean it. I never should've spilled anything. Now remove your sulky bones from my room – I have revising to do.'

2

Liccle Bit's Warning

Liccle Bit slapped on my gates the next morning at 7.50 a.m.

I had been up most of the night. I didn't want to kick Liccle Bit into the stress zone, but I was meant to be his number-one bredren. *If I was Liccle Bit I'd want to know if Manjaro was alive and breathing Crongton air. I'm scared for him. Heather will curse my toes, but I have to leak the breaking news to Liccle Bit.*

Mum had already left for work. Dad was being proper miserable in his bedroom. Heather sipped a hot chocolate at the breakfast table while checking her phone messages and I had toasted the last two slices of bread.

Liccle Bit zoomed straight for the kitchen and parked his short butt opposite Heather. A messed-up grin spread from his cheeks.

'Hi, Heather.' Liccle Bit's voice was deeper than usual. 'What's going on?'

Heather flicked a glance at Bit. She acknowledged him with a half grunt before returning her gaze to her phone.

'Let's step,' I said to Bit and collected my school rucksack.

We jumped down three steps at a time. When we reached ground level, we looked across to McKay's slab to see him hot-stepping towards us as if a peckish Godzilla wanted to snack on him.

'I've seen an elephant fly,' joked Bit. 'And watched crocodiles twerking on YouTube. But man has *never* seen McKay sprint at this time of morning.'

McKay huffed and puffed and finally reached us. His cheeks wobbled as he bent over and gripped his knees. For a short second I tried to remember my CPR training. McKay's school bag hung off one shoulder. 'Breaking news!' he gasped. He blew out another three long exhales before he spoke again. I thought he was gonna capsize. 'Breaking news!'

'Are you about to have a heart attack?' asked Bit. 'Or bust a fart?'

'You forgot the cooking oil for your fried eggs this morning?' I added.

McKay shook his head. 'It's much more serious than that,' he said. 'I'm not playing. Manjaro has been seen in the ends.'

'Stop lying, bruv,' said Bit. 'If I had a strawberry cheesecake every time someone told me they'd seen

Manjaro, I'd be sumo wrestling right now.'

'I'm not lying, bro,' said McKay. 'The guy who has seen him goes to that Seventh-Day Adventist Church on Crongton Hill. Them people can't lie.'

Liccle Bit laughed. 'So, you're telling me that because this bruv attends a Seventh-Day Adventist Church, he's telling the truth?'

'Yep.' McKay nodded. 'As I said, it's impossible for them to lie. If they do, they get sent to Greenland or Antarctica. They have to spread the gospel to polar bears, penguins, yetis and igloo folk.'

'What's a yeti?' I asked.

'A Bigfoot,' replied McKay.

'What's a Bigfoot?' I wanted to know.

'Don't you guys watch *Unexplained Mysteries?*' wondered McKay. 'A Bigfoot is like that snow monster in *Star Wars: Episode V*. They live up in the mountains. And they munch on peeps who wanna reach the mountain peak.'

'McKay.' Liccle Bit raised his voice. 'Stop chatting foolishness.'

'It's not foolishness,' I said. 'My sis said the same ting about the Manjaro situation. She heard it at that save-the-youth-club-building meeting.'

'Hard kerb rumours,' said Bit. 'In a thousand years' time, peeps will still be saying they seen Manjaro here and saw him there.'

'My sis wouldn't lie,' I said.

'But did she see Manjaro herself?'

'Er, no,' I replied. 'Not exactly.'

'Then stop trying to give me sweats and let's trod to school,' said Bit.

He started towards school. McKay and I swapped a glance before catching up with him.

'What's all this about Heather and peeps trying to save the old youth club building?' Bit asked.

'I think they're trying to raise some Gs so they can nice-up the building and reopen it,' I replied.

'Tell Heather that I'll help if there's any liccle ting I can do,' said Bit.

'Bit's only asking cos Heather has always tickled his fancy buttons,' said McKay. 'That's the dirty truth of the situation. You know it!'

'What's wrong with you, bruv?' I raised my voice to Bit. 'I told you already, she's not gonna walk on street linking arms and slobbering tongues with someone who's a liccle pup to her. Not gonna happen. I don't think she would even go out with a bro who's four months younger than her, let alone four years. And anyways, you're too damn short and you're with Venetia. Don't be greedy, bruv.'

'I've grown five centimetres in seven months,' said Bit. 'I'm in the middle of a growth spurt. And I'm not greedy.'

'You're damn greedy!' I snapped. 'And even if you were single and in Heather's age range, you'd have about as much chance with her as an ant in a waterfall.'

'That's cold,' said McKay. 'By the way, what's the Venetia situation?'

Bit refused to answer, shook his head and stepped on ahead. I answered for him. 'Venetia's still vexed that Bit watched me run at Crongton Heath Rec two weeks ago instead of seeing her dance at that school show. She was pissed with a big P.'

'She's still cussing about that?' McKay asked.

'Yep,' I replied. 'Didn't you hear them warring in the playground the other day?'

'Nope,' replied McKay.

'Venetia was saying that Bit always put his friends before her,' I revealed. 'They haven't chatted since. All's not good in Bit and Venetia's paradise.'

'So that's why he's trying to hit on my sis,' I laughed.

Ahead of us, Bit slowed down. He waited for me and McKay to catch up. 'I'll have to chat to Venetia today,' he said. 'And give her the score about Manjaro.'

'Manjaro,' I repeated. 'It's like that bruv is haunting us.'

'He's probably dead,' said Bit. 'Maybe Major Worries finally deleted him. Maybe the feds haven't found his body yet. The kerb-bangers in our ends have been on the low-profile tip for a long time now. If Manjaro was alive or in the ends my sis would've heard about it.'

'I hope you're right,' said McKay.

I nodded. 'Me too.'

3

Mr Smallwood

My school morning went on all good until Wilson McKenzie spotted me in the science lab corridors. 'Look,' he laughed. 'It's the food-bank kid! What are you munching tonight, Jonah? Pilchards on stale bread? Cornflakes on water? Acorn soup?'

Morgan Stapleton! He needs to self-isolate his mouth for a century or two.

'At least when I'm on holiday I can actually sight the sea instead of the Crongton wilderness like your fam do,' I retaliated. 'We don't do staycations in shoebox-size caravans.'

'Maybe so, but I'm sampling a lamb shank dinner tonight,' Wilson said. 'With organic baby potatoes, a liccle mint on top and veg that doesn't come out of a can. I'd invite you round but I don't wanna take you away from your tinned fish in that creamy tomatoness. Poor folk say it's proper delicious.'

'Ignore him,' said McKay. 'Come, let's roll to drama.'

Half an hour later, Saira, McKay and I were performing this little sketch about a girl who was just about to tell her parents that she was a lesbian. It was Saira's idea. I played the mum and McKay took the dad role.

It was good to do something gigglelicious. I was just about to deliver my first line when Smallwood bounced in. He said a quick apology to our drama teacher, Ms Halle Dandridge, who did not look impressed, before swinging over to me. 'Enjoying yourself, Jonah?'

'Er, yeah,' I replied.

'Can you see me after school? In my office.'

'Yeah. OK.'

'Can they do their sketch now?' Ms Dandridge cut in. '*We* don't intervene when you take your PE lessons, do we?'

'I'm sorry,' Smallwood apologised. 'It's important.'

'I should hope so,' Ms Dandridge replied.

As Smallwood left the drama studio, Ms Dandridge adjusted the long rainbow-coloured scarf around her neck – I couldn't tell you how many times she had tripped over that thing.

'It's not looking sweet for Venetia and Bit.' Saira parked beside me on the floor after our sketch. 'Can't you chat to Bit and get him to say sorry?'

Mr Smallwood

'Me?' I replied. 'I'm not getting involved with a bredren's love business. Don't wanna get burned. I didn't tell Bit he had to watch me run. He just turned up.'

'Jonah!' Saira raised her voice. 'You know them two are a proper match. But they're stubborn like mules with attitude. One of them's gonna have to climb down from their Mount Pride. Can't you tweet a word in Bit's ear corner? You know, help get them back together? I'm working on Venetia.'

'Oh, all right,' I agreed. 'But I have to see Smallwood after school. I'll slap on Bit's gates this evening.'

'Thanks,' said Saira. 'If those two repair tings, your next cheesecake's on me.'

'I want that in writing,' I said. 'And it has to be the raspberry ripple super-duper one.'

'What about me?' McKay cut in. 'Don't I love cheesecake too? Especially the raspberry ripple super-duper. I'll chase that mother down with a South Crongton kerb-island iced tea.'

'A South Crongton kerb-island iced tea?' repeated Saira. 'Never heard of it.'

'Nor have I,' laughed McKay. 'But I'm gonna invent it.'

My last lesson of the day was history. Ms James was going on all serious about the French revolution. It seemed as if she proper loved talking about royal folk getting deleted in X-rated ways. I liked the guillotine bit, but I spent most of the lesson scoping the classroom clock. Why did Smallwood want to see me? When the buzzer sounded, I was the first out into the corridor. I made my way to the PE department and smacked on Smallwood's door.

'Come in.'

I pushed the door open.

The room reeked of the kinda sweat you saw in the last round of a heavyweight boxing fight.

Smallwood sat his big self behind a small untidy desk. Basketballs, footballs, hockey balls, lacrosse sticks and badminton racquets cluttered the floor. It was a victory to get his crusty self behind the desk. Hung on the wall behind him were certificates and school team photos of various sports. I spotted myself in a photo of the Year 8 athletics squad taken just before the regional championships. At that meet I came third in the two hundred metres.

Smallwood had long thinning black hair and ancient sideburns. He looked like the lead singer of a 1970s band that my dad liked to watch. His grey-blue eyes were close together. Some students called him Hawkman.

'Close the door and sit down,' he said.

When I did what I was told, he leaned forward and rested his chin on a fat fist.

'Is something up?' he asked. 'Everything all right at home?'

'Yeah, course,' I replied. 'Everything's sweet.'

'You sure?' Smallwood pressed.

'Yeah, I'm double sure,' I said and scratched my nose.

Mr Smallwood

Smallwood looked at me with hard eyes.

'Your times still haven't recovered,' he said. 'Three months ago, you were running over a second quicker than you are now. When I first brought it up you said you'd work on it. Any explanation?'

'Er, just been very busy – you know how school goes. Bags of revising.'

'Any injury?'

'Nope.'

'Are you sure everything's all right at home?' he asked again. 'Your dad OK?'

'Yeah, he's good,' I replied, wondering why he'd asked about Dad.

Maybe he knows Pops is unemployed. I can't spill that I haven't been sleeping too well. He'd want to know why and make me fill in untold forms.

'Performances can drop off if the athlete is stressed about something,' he said. 'And as a teacher, we have to look out for changes in behaviour.'

I shrugged. 'I'm good,' I lied. 'Nothing's stressing me out. All's ripe cheesecakes in my world.'

'Cheesecakes?' Smallwood raised his eyebrows. 'You want to watch what you eat. You're training to be an elite athlete.' Smallwood knitted his fingers together and leaned a bit closer. It was hard to escape his intense stare. 'You have it in you to reach the top,' he said. 'And I'm not just talking about British level. I'm talking about the Diamond League, the World Championships. The Olympics.'

I smiled. 'Yeah, that's what I dream about. I hope one day a gold medal's gonna bless my chest.'

'But you have to focus and *not* let up in your training,' Smallwood said. 'Gold medals cost, and it starts with dedication. Are you sure that life hasn't given you a nudge? Knocked you off course? Do you know what I mean?'

I looked at the papers on Smallwood's desk. I tried to read one of them upside down.

'Jonah? Are you listening to me?'

'Yeah, course I'm listening.'

'I'm here for you,' he said. 'If there's anything bothering you, just knock on my door and we can have a confidential chat.'

'If there's anything *troubling* me, you'll be the first to know,' I said. 'Trust me on that one.'

Smallwood nodded. 'Are you free Saturday morning?'

'Yeah, I think so.'

'Good, so I'll see you on the Heath at nine-thirty. We need to work on your stamina. Your first three hundred is always excellent but you're dropping off in the last hundred metres.'

'I'm there.'

'Good,' said Smallwood.

'Can I go now?'

'Yes, you can.' I turned to leave.

'Before you go . . .' Smallwood's words stopped me but I didn't turn around. 'You have so much potential, Jonah,' Smallwood said. 'It's my job to see that you fulfil it.

I wouldn't want you to waste it for whatever reason.'

'I'm on it, sir,' I replied. 'Trust me on that.'

'Have a look at this.' Smallwood stood up and climbed over all the balls, sticks and racquets on the floor. He took out his phone from his back pocket and held it under my nose. 'Michael Johnson at the 1996 Atlanta Olympics in the four-hundred final.' Smallwood grinned. 'Probably the greatest four-hundred-metre runner in history.'

He pressed play on the screen.

Camera lights and flashes lit up the Olympic stadium.

With his upright running style, Michael Johnson burned around the track. I liked the gold chain he wore around his neck. I made a mental note to style one when I'm in a major final. The crowd hollered and roared as he approached the finish line. His rivals were barely in the same camera shot.

Smallwood paused the video. He caught me in another long glare.

'That could be you,' he said. 'Can you imagine it? All that cheering. People you've never met wanting your autograph. They'll put a gold postbox in South Crongton in your honour. That would be something. *Don't* waste your talent.'

'I won't,' I replied.

'Next time I'll show you a Cuban runner called Alberto Juantorena.'

'Alberto who? He sounds like a drink.'

'He's certainly not a drink,' Smallwood said. 'You'll see.'

I opened the door and left.

For a short while, I sat in the empty changing room near to Smallwood's office. I didn't really want to roll home yet nor try to sort out Liccle Bit's love business. I heard the yelps and shouts from the girls' Year 10 basketball team practising in the gym. I peered through the gym window and wondered if any of them had the potential to make it in elite sport.

If I had a bag of money right now, I'd pay off all our debts, Mum wouldn't have to boot Pops outta the yard and my sis wouldn't need to find a part-time job. If there was any change left, I'd bless my feet with the name-brand spikes that Usain Bolt wears.

The corridors were empty and quiet, and as I left the school gates, I wondered what I could say to Liccle Bit to get him to apologise to Venetia. Then I thought about the raspberry ripple super-duper cheesecake that Saira had promised me. I licked my lips and could almost taste the deliciousness of the fruit sliding down my throat. *It's been too long since I had a cheesecake treat. Better not let Smallwood see me sampling—*

Someone blocked the pavement.

I looked up.

Shit times five!

4

The General's Lair

He was so wide that cars might've mistaken him for a roundabout. His blue baseball cap strained to fit on his Millennium-Dome-sized head. His blue T-shirt was taut like a mega-sized elastic band. A well-skilled barber designed his eyebrows, landscaped his chin and sideburns. A diamond stud niced up his left ear. His eyes locked on me like an assassin's rifle. Dread sprinted through every artery of my body.

I couldn't move.

I shifted my eyes and prayed for witnesses.

'Get in the ride,' said Mr Dome-Head.

On the other side of the road, a woman walked her small dog. He was sniffing a skinny tree stump. He then lifted his hind leg and took a piss. I hoped she'd turn around and look at my petrified self. I thought about screaming. *Bad idea*.

'Don't let me repeat myself,' said Mr Dome-Head. 'Get your bones in the car.'

I dared to look up and noticed that he had a scar below his left ear that ran down to his left armpit. I wondered who on this sweet earth would even think about carving him. His shoulders seemed wide enough to span the Mississippi. Parked just behind him was a bruised-black Volkswagen Golf. The engine hummed. The windows were tinted. My phone vibrated in my pocket, but I didn't reach for it.

'We're not gonna hurt you,' said Mr Dome-Head. 'Trust me, that's not on our agenda.'

My blood flowed again. I started towards the car. Mr Dome-Head opened the back door for me.

I took a breath and stepped in. I sniffed something nice. It almost made me sneeze. Grime beats played on the car stereo. My seat was comfy. Mr Dome-Head got in beside me. When he parked his butt, I almost bounced up to the car ceiling. My heartbeat had a frantic African drumming moment.

I looked ahead.

A female driver. Twenty, maybe twenty-one. She was white with a Mediterranean tan.

Something blinged from her earlobes. *Diamonds?* Sky-blue highlights sexed up her blonde hair. She wore skinny sunglasses. Purple lipstick. As pretty as a Bond chick. A lion tattoo roared on her left hand. At least I thought it roared. On her other wrist she styled a gold watch with a dark face.

'Don't fret yourself,' she said as she pushed into first gear. 'No blade's gonna prick your skin. The general wants to chat to you.'

'Who . . . who's the general?' I wanted to know.

Suddenly, everything went dark.

Mr Dome-Head covered my head with a Footcave bag.

'Don't delete me!' I panicked. 'I don't mingle with any kerb-bangers. I'm just a kid who goes to school. I don't get involved in any shit—'

My breathing hit fifth gear.

I didn't suffer from asthma but wondered if this was what an attack felt like.

'Relax, my speedy yout,' said Mr Dome-Head. 'Just taking precautions. What you can't see, you can't tell.'

I felt the sway of the car as it turned corners and navigated bends. We drove straight at a good speed for a quarter of an hour or so before we caught up in traffic again. *Maybe we're on the Crongton Circular? Liccle Bit, McKay, Saira, Venetia and Boy from the Hills are not gonna believe this one.*

We turned left into a quiet street. The driver reversed into a parking spot. Birds twittered. Soft breezes passed through leaves. I heard an ice cream van in the distance. I sniffed the air. *Someone's having curry this evening. Another family feasting on kebab. I might be deleted tonight! Worms will be sucking out my eyes. Caterpillars will be licking my toenails. Mum, Dad and Heather will be crying lakes at my funeral. McKay will be asking for seconds. Bugs will be crawling up my nose corners. My parents aren't too bad. And Heather's a good sister. She bought me my first spikes for my last birthday. She comes to see me run when she can. Hope I'll see them again.*

'What are you gonna do with me?' I asked. 'My parents are expecting me home quick-time after school. The woman with the dog saw me climbing into your ride.'

No answer.

Mr Dome-Head opened a door for me. He led me out and guided me on to the pavement. 'You're stepping down, my speedy yout. Be careful.'

How does he know that I'm speedy?

I counted five steps. Mr Dome-Head pulled me left. I heard the crunch of a mortice key. A solid bolt was pulled back.

The door opened with a long creak.

It might be a cellar. I'm gonna end my days where spiders and bugs hang out. There's gonna be hooks and long nails in the brick walls. Blobs and dribbles of blood might be dripping from the ceiling. A chainsaw might be waiting for me.

Mr Dome-Head placed his big hand on the back of my right shoulder and gently pushed me inside.

I sniffed something.

Mince? Meatballs? Spaghetti?

The heat of a cooker hit my cheeks. The door was shut behind me. I heard the lock click into place. Mr Dome-Head pulled off the Footcave bag.

The wooden-tiled flooring was mahogany-brown. It was clean and very neat.

The General's Lair

There was a man stirring something in the kitchen. He had a bald head. Five foot nine, maybe five foot ten. He wore a loose-fitting blue tracksuit. A small gold cross glinted from his left ear. On the index finger of his left hand he wore a ring with a black onyx star set in a gold mount. I couldn't make out the tattoo on his neck. He didn't seem to notice my presence as he continued to stir a mince pot, a tea towel draped over his right shoulder. On a shelf, a small digital radio blared out some old school R&B. The driver took off her skinny sunglasses and parked in an armchair in the corner of the room. Her eyes were greeny-blue. She took out her phone and scrolled. She looked as cool as a polar bear relaxing in a Jacuzzi. Mr Dome-Head stood by the side door that led up to ground level.

No escape.

A fold-up bed was pressed against the far wall.

I realised I was in a bedsit.

'Are you hungry, my rapid yout?' the man mixing the food asked.

I recognised him. There was no mistake.

Manjaro.

I felt my roast-beef school lunch come to life again. I thought about all the peeps he had deleted. Fed sirens blared in my head. Hospital operating theatres gate-crashed my mind.

I took in a long breath. *I love my family.*

'Er . . .' I replied. 'No, er, yeah, I'm a liccle bit peckish.'

'Sit down,' he ordered. 'There's a stool over there. Let's chat.'

He pointed to a black leather barstool by the fridge. I went over to it and sat down. I nearly tipped over and lost my balance.

'Five more minutes I reckon,' Manjaro said, studying his mince pot. 'The tomato's bubbling sweetly. The spaghetti's ripe.'

I couldn't help being drawn by his huge black star ring.

'Why... why have you got me here?' I wanted to know. 'I'm not a kerbman. I don't involve myself in any kerb-banging business. I go to church with my mum.'

I hadn't attended a service for more than three years.

'I know, I know,' Manjaro said. 'I also know that you're Liccle Bit's best bredren.'

'Yeah.' I nodded. 'I've known Liccle Bit for all of my days. We live in the same slab.'

Manjaro stirred the pot again. He took out a teaspoon from a drawer and tasted the mince. He smiled. 'It's ready,' he said. 'Just enough garlic and seasoning. Do you want some grated cheese on yours? I've got a slab of mild cheddar.'

Did the most feared G in South Crong just offer me mild cheddar cheese?

I nodded.

Manjaro collected four dinner plates from a cupboard. He placed them on a small round table in the middle of the room. Knives and forks were already set. There was a large

The General's Lair

bottle of water and a can of beer. 'Everyone, take your seats,' he said.

Mr Dome-Head, Miss Cool and Manjaro sat around the table. I joined them. I wondered if it would be my last meal. I said a quick prayer to every god I had heard of as Manjaro poured water into glasses. Mr Dome-Head claimed the beer.

I couldn't lie – the mince was good. It had the proper amount of tomato flavour in it. McKay would've given it top ratings. The spaghetti was just right. I curled it around my fork. I chased it down with cold water. *Maybe I should pour it over my head to cool my nerves down.*

'To answer your question of why you're here,' Manjaro said, 'let me explain. I'll be . . . going away for a while. This little basement flat is all right for what I need, but I'll go cadazy if I spend another week in here. It's getting boring. I wake up in the morning wondering what to do with myself. I've had too much time on my hands. Life is for living.'

'Wh . . . Where're you going?' I asked.

'You'll soon find out,' Manjaro replied.

'Why do you want me here?' I wanted to know.

Manjaro looked up to the ceiling and thought about it. I took another sip of water. It was freezing cold.

Manjaro began. 'I have set up Lady P and Pinchers here to run my tings while I'm away. I hope Pinchers didn't scare you too tough when he asked you to join me.'

'No . . . no, he didn't,' I said. 'Not . . . not at all.'

Pinchers sank a monster mouthful of mince and spaghetti. I imagined him to be a T. rex munching on a cow. Lady P checked her phone again.

'I wanted to set up my son, Jerome,' Manjaro said. 'You know that Liccle Bit's sis has a baby for me, right?'

'Yeah, I know that. Jerome. He's cute. Very cute.'

'I want to set him up neatly,' explained Manjaro. 'Set up a trust fund or leave him a legacy. When he comes of age maybe he could use the Gs to set up his own business or someting. But, Elaine . . . she's not feeling that. She doesn't want a penny of grime from me.'

'Oh,' I said. 'That's . . .'

'That's unfortunate,' Manjaro said. 'She doesn't want me to involve Liccle Bit. It's understandable. I did terrorise him and his grandma. I own that shit and know it was well wrong. I wasn't in a good zone back then. I've apologised nuff times to Elaine. She's . . . she's not hearing me.'

'Wh . . . where do I come into this?'

Manjaro finished his glass of water. He placed it down on the table. He swapped a glance with Lady P. Pinchers grabbed his can of beer. As he took a glug his neck muscles bulged like rugby balls in a Christmas stocking.

'I'm gonna give you a choice,' Manjaro said. 'A simple choice. It's up to you if you wanna take it or not.'

'Wh . . . what kinda choice?'

'To take an envelope or to not take an envelope.'

'Huh?' I asked. 'What do you mean?'

'What would you do if you had a big bag of money?' Manjaro asked.

'Help my parents out,' I replied. 'Give something to my sis. If it was a massive bag of Gs I'd share it with my best bredrens—'

'Ah!' Manjaro cut me off. 'I knew you'd say that. So, you'd give a portion to Liccle Bit. And you should give him at least half, cos if it wasn't for him you wouldn't be given this opportunity.'

'Yeah, of course,' I said. 'I've known him since year dot.'

'I like that.' Manjaro nodded. 'You're a socialist at heart.'

'I'm a what?'

'A socialist,' Manjaro repeated. 'What do you think Liccle Bit would do if he had a pile of notes?'

'Spend it on his family,' I replied.

'Yes!' Manjaro raised his voice. He stood up and punched the air. 'Correct answer! He'll probably use most of it to spoil his nephew. I'm not gonna lie – I'd love that. I'd appreciate it even more if the funds were used to set tings up for your future.'

'Most Crongton folk would share Gs with family,' I said.

'The important ting is –' Manjaro sat back down – 'you like to share. Liccle Bit likes to share. That's how it should be. There's not enough sharing in our ends.'

'So what?' I asked. 'You're giving me a big envelope with nuff Gs inside it?'

'Not exactly,' Manjaro replied. 'I don't like giving my hard-fought funds to the uneducated. And let me emphasise *hard*-fought. You know how it goes on the Crongton kerbs.'

Pinchers and Lady P nodded.

'You'll have to use your hard drive and work for the Gs,' added Manjaro. '*Earn* it. Nothing comes easy in this mad life. You think the profit I've got came easy? I had to wet a few necks.'

'N . . . no,' I replied. 'How? How do I earn it?'

'It's all in the envelope. You might learn something as well.'

'How much? Learn what?'

Manjaro laughed a wild laugh. An image of those cadazy hyenas in *The Lion King* burst into my head. He swapped another glance with Lady P. 'That's for you to find out,' he said. He leaned towards me. 'And the only way you can find out is by taking the envelope. All I will tell you is that my fave subject in school was history.'

I thought about it. *Liccle Bit leaked to me once that Manjaro owns houses and shit. It could be fifty grand. Maybe a hundred Gs! Heather wouldn't have to find a part-time job. I could get my name-brand spikes. I could take a cab to Crongton Heath for training every other day. I'd buy Liccle Bit and McKay any footwear they wanted. Might get them the latest tablets if they proper appreciate it. I'd take Saira to the Shenk-I-Sheck club. I hope they'd let me in.*

Manjaro dabbed his mouth with a tissue. 'I'm going to take a piss,' he said. 'By the time I come back, I'd like an answer. Do you want the envelope or not? Simple.'

The General's Lair

My heartbeat walloped my tonsils. *It's not like a Liccle Bit situation. He's not asking me to carry a gun or sell any dragon-hip pills. He's not inviting me to join his crew and he hasn't ordered me to shank a North Crong kerbman.*

He's just asking me to take an envelope. How wrong could this go? When I get home, I could burn it and forget about it.

Pinchers stood up, collected his plate and washed it up in the sink. Lady P texted somebody. For a short second I thought about hot-toeing outta there. But my curiosity drop-kicked my common sense.

Manjaro had been in the toilet for five minutes, but it seemed like five hours. He returned and filled his seat. He topped off his glass with water and looked at me. His eyes narrowed. 'What will it be?' he asked.

'Er...' I replied. 'Could... could I change my mind? And if I do, nothing would happen to me?'

Manjaro seized me with a glare. For the first time in his presence, I sensed a menacing impatience in him. 'If I wanted to trouble you, do you think you'd be still conscious?'

I shook my head. 'No.'

'I'll give you my South Crong word,' Manjaro added. 'No one in this room will even trouble a liccle hair 'pon your headtop.'

'That's... good,' I managed. 'Good to know.'

Manjaro opened a kitchen drawer. He took out a gold envelope. It was pristine with not a crease, and half the size of an A4 page. There wasn't a name on it nor an address.

'Keep it safe,' said Manjaro. 'Peeps would pay good money for this. You wouldn't want it to get in the wrong hands.'

He slid it across the table to me. I picked it up. There didn't seem to be much inside. Maybe one page.

'Put it inside your bag now,' Manjaro advised. 'Don't lose it. I spent a lot of my good time on it.'

I did what I was told under the watchful eyes of Lady P and Pinchers.

'All right, my speedy yout.' Manjaro stood up again. 'I don't know if we will meet again. Have you ever read *Treasure Island*? Or seen a film version?'

'Er, no,' I replied.

'That was my fave book as a kid,' Manjaro said. 'My dad used to read it to me. It was the only positive ting he ever done for me.'

Silence.

Manjaro was lost in his thoughts for a few moments. I wondered who his pops was or if he was still alive.

'If you find my treasure, you would've earned it,' Manjaro resumed. 'And learned something too. But mind your step, my speedy yout – there's nuff Long John Silvers out there.'

I couldn't help but think of gold coins, diamond bracelets and wads of cash.

Manjaro looked at Lady P and communicated something with his eyes. Lady P stood up, put on her slim sunglasses and searched for her car keys inside her lizard-skinned handbag. She looked at me. 'Come,' she said.

The General's Lair

I moved towards the door. Before I got there, Pinchers turned my day into night again by covering my head with the Footcave bag.

They escorted me to the ride.

On the return journey, Lady P played some jazz on the car stereo. It didn't soothe my nerves. With the gold envelope in it, my bag seemed much heavier.

They dropped me off close to my school.

'Do you need some bus fare?' Lady P asked. 'Or a travel card?'

'No,' I replied.

'All right, my rapid yout,' Pinchers said. 'Trod safely.'

Lady P drove off. I watched her car disappear into the distance before I made my first step.

Burning racetracks! Do I spill to Liccle Bit? Leak to the feds? Or keep this shit to myself? Cancel the feds idea – Pinchers' fists are too large. What am I gonna do? Maybe tell Heather? Nah, she will just cuss my behind for climbing into Lady P's ride. And my parents don't need this drama on top of their issues either.

I checked my phone.

There was a message from Saira.

Have you chatted to Liccle Bit yet? I'm working on Venetia.

I almost forgot.

5

Manjaro's Code

I jogged back to my slab. I planned on changing my clothes first before slapping on Liccle Bit's gates. Before I reached home concrete, I spotted Liccle Bit and Venetia in the children's play area behind my block. Venetia sat on one of the swings and Bit stood nearby staring at the ground. Venetia's tones weren't happy. When I bounced up to them they didn't even notice me.

'It's not just about you not turning up to see my dance performance after school.' Venetia raised her voice to Bit. '*Three* times I've invited you to come up to my yard and each time you've come up with a crappy excuse.'

'But—' Liccle Bit managed.

'But *nothing!*' Venetia cut him off. 'Look how many times I've come to your flat. I've lost count. It's been about twice a week since we've been linking. I know your grandma's story inside out cos I spend nuff time with her. I know that your sis bought your liccle nephew some new clothes the other day cos I was there when Jerome was trying them on. I know that your mum is pissed off with her job. What do you know about my fam?'

'Er... your dad is one of the speakers at the church... and—'

'Is that it?' snapped Venetia. 'Does my yard stink? Don't you like our food? Have you got someting against my parents?'

'No, no!' Bit shook his head. 'It's not that. Your parents are cool.'

'Is it because they're church folk?' Venetia kept pushing. 'And because we say grace before every meal? I heard you say to McKay that my fam is in the God squad. *Liberties!*'

'It's not that either. My grandma goes to their same church.'

'Then what?'

Bit side-eyed me. Venetia sensed me too, but she blazed her eyes on Bit once more. 'Answer the question!' she insisted. 'What is it that keeps you away from my yard?'

'Your... your pops.'

'What about my pops?' she demanded to know.

'He... he's always staring at me as if he wants to koof me into a different orbit.'

I almost giggled. I placed a hand over my mouth.

'What? You're being ridiculous,' said Venetia.

'No, I'm not,' argued Bit. 'Your pops is... proper

intimidating. He's . . . he's not small. And a betting man wouldn't know who to put his Gs on if your pops clashed with the Hulk in the ring.'

'My pops is one of the gentlest people in our ends,' Venetia insisted. 'He's never raised a knuckle to anyone.'

Bit glanced at me. 'Jonah!'

'Jonah,' Venetia repeated. 'We're just having a liccle issue. Bear with us. Won't be long.'

'And when I wanna do someting with you,' added Bit to Venetia. 'Like go to the movies or the Cheesecake Lounge, you're always busy with your dancing or doing someting with Saira. When's the last time we had me-and-you time?'

Venetia's attention returned to Bit. I felt the heat from her eyes where I stood. 'You're meant to support me in my dancing,' she said to him. 'You're my boyfriend, so you're meant to back me in *everything*. You know how important it is to me. But when I'm not doing anyting, you can't even come to my yard and spend time with my fam.'

'Your pops don't even like me sitting next to you,' Bit said. 'He'd probably fling me over your balcony if I kissed you on the cheek. And you're on the seventh floor. My liccle body will be a gooey mess when it connects with the hard concrete.'

Venetia shook her head and offered Bit one of her most brutal eye-passes.

'You know what,' she said. 'If you can't respect me

enough to come to my yard, then I'm not stepping to your slab. End of. I'll only see you at school.'

'Wha . . . what do you mean, "end of"?' Bit asked.

Venetia pointed at me. 'Try to work it out next time you watch him run!'

Venetia stood up, gave Bit one more bad-ass side-eye and marched off like Bit had busted the world's smelliest fart.

'That was ferocious,' I said to Bit. 'Why didn't you just go to her yard?'

'You don't know her pops,' Bit replied. 'He watches my every move and sniffs my every breath. I feel that if I so much as put my arm around her, he will munch it off and lick me with it.'

'He can't be that bad,' I said.

Bit gave me a look that told me I was well wrong.

I parked on the swing that Venetia had vacated. 'Got something I wanna chat to you about,' I said.

'About your parents?' Bit guessed. 'The whole slab knows they're having their issues. My mum heard them cussing each other today when we were at school.'

'No, it's not that—'

'Jonah, you're my best bredren, but I don't wanna hear it right now,' Bit cut me off. 'It looks as if Venetia's booted me to the kerb, Elaine's been picking on me in the last few weeks and my artwork has not been up to spec. Stress is stroking me *hard*. We'll chat tomorrow if I'm in a better zone.' He loped off with his head bowed.

I felt sorry for him. *How can I bring up the Manjaro situation now? What to do? What to do? Gotta tell somebody. This gold envelope's well heavy. Saira always has good advice. Let me ding her. Nah. Rewind that. She'll spill to Venetia. I don't need that drama.*

I took out my phone and dinged McKay.

'Jonah,' McKay answered. 'What's bubbling?'

'Where are you?' I asked.

'I'm at Boy from the Hills' yard,' McKay replied. 'We're shooting pool and sinking some serious chow mein.'

'I need to chat to you about someting,' I said. 'But keep it on the low profile.'

'Need to chat about what?' McKay wanted to know. 'I don't wanna hear about your wanking issues.'

I heard Boy from the Hills giggling in the background.

'It's serious,' I said. 'Well serious.'

'So, you can't spill to me on the phone?' McKay wondered.

'Er, no,' I said. 'This is MI5, CIA-high-command confidential.'

'Then slap on your spikes and set your gears to Boy from the Hills' yard.'

'OK,' I said. 'I'll be up there in half an hour or so.'

'Coolio,' said McKay. 'Are you sure it's not wanking issues? You haven't sprained yourself have you? Accidents can happen.'

'*No!* I'm frickin sure,' I replied. 'Can't a man ever be serious?'

I killed the call and dinged Mum to tell her I was gonna see a friend before I landed home.

'I've cooked rice and fish,' Mum said. 'When you come home, *don't* waste it!'

I arrived at Boy from the Hills' mansion twenty-five minutes later. No cars were in the curved gravel driveway, so I guessed his parents weren't at home. I thumbed the doorbell and scoped the front lawn. The two cherry trees had reached full blossom and pinked up the scene. The hedges and bushes were neatly trimmed like a bad boy's beard. The South Crongton hills were in the distance. I inspected the front of the house. Seemed as if they had painted the place yesterday. *Gosh! A window cleaner could spend a whole morning doing his thing.*

Boy from the Hills opened the double front door – you could drive a four-by-four through it. He held a pool cue in his hands. His hair looked as if fat bees, monkeys and eagles were having a ferocious war in there.

'Jonah,' he greeted me. 'Come, you can play the winner.'

I followed him into the house. I had been there before, but I couldn't help being impressed by the short spiral staircase in the hallway and the weird paintings on the walls. Boy from the Hills once told me his mum was into cubism. Liccle Bit knew what he was rapping about, but I didn't have a diddly.

The dining room had a table that seated twelve. Blue orchids were in a fancy glass pot in the middle. Boy from the Hills told me he never ate there. The kitchen had a kidney-shaped marble island in the centre. The fridge could've housed a family of Inuits and a pet wolf.

He led me downstairs to the basement. It had a card-playing table with a green felt cloth surface in the corner of the room. On the other side they had one of those ancient jukeboxes with vinyl records. Portraits and paintings of sports stars covered three walls, including Muhammad Ali, a basketball player I'd never heard of called Kareem Abdul-Jabbar, Pelé, Bobby Moore, Ian Botham, Viv Richards and some tennis player called Arthur Ashe. A cinema screen filled the fourth wall. I made a mental note to reserve my seat when the next Olympics came around.

There was a bar with every kind of drink you could think of. Two empty takeaway cartons rested on the counter with a couple of extra-large cups of Coca-Cola. In the middle of the space was a pool table. The blue playing cloth looked as if somebody had dry-cleaned it.

McKay lined up a shot. 'Jonah!' he hailed me. 'You wanna play the winner?'

'Er . . . maybe,' I replied.

McKay missed the shot. Boy from the Hills studied the table, chalked his cue and then cleaned up. I can't lie – he was damn good.

McKay offered me his stick. 'So, what's your drama?' he asked.

'Er . . .'

I hesitated as Boy from the Hills set up the balls in a triangle.

'What?' McKay said. 'You hot-stepped all the way up here to tell us zero?'

'No, no,' I replied.

'Then what's the breaking news?' Boy from the Hills pressed.

I placed the cue down on the pool table. I parked myself on a black leather barstool.

'Manjaro,' I revealed.

'You've seen him?' McKay wanted to know. 'He's alive?'

'You heard something?' Boy from the Hills asked.

'They found his body?'

'The feds got him?'

'Elaine deleted him?'

'He's merked another North Crong kerbman?'

'No, no,' I replied. 'None of that. I was kidnapped. I was taken to his hideout.'

I spilled the whole story from when Pinchers ordered me to get into the car until Lady P dropped me off near my school. I took out the gold envelope and placed it on the pool table. Boy from the Hills and McKay looked at it as if it might explode.

'Open it!' urged Boy from the Hills.

'You open it,' I said.

'I don't want my fingerprints on it,' said Boy from the Hills. 'The word on the kerbs says Manjaro deleted *three* men. And probably ordered another ten to be shanked.'

In The Ends

'Rolling doughnuts!' said McKay. 'What's a matter with you? It's only a fricking envelope!'

'Then you open it,' I said.

McKay picked up the envelope and examined it like it was a lost chapter from the Bible. I spotted a bottle of Coke on the bar and went over to pour myself a cup. I made it a large one. It bubbled up neatly.

McKay opened the envelope and a folded page dropped out along with a black star that seemed to be cut from felt.

'What does it say?' Boy from the Hills asked. 'Are there any instructions? Is there some kinda code on it? Will it self-combust in thirty seconds? I wonder what the black star means?'

McKay picked up the black star and studied it. I remembered the ring Manjaro wore on his index finger.

'Shouldn't Liccle Bit be here for this?' I asked.

'Manjaro gave the envelope to you,' McKay said. 'Bit's not in a good zone cos of the Venetia situation. We'll tell him later.'

McKay unfolded the page. Someone had typed a short paragraph. It was in bold italics.

'Read it then,' urged Boy from the Hills. 'What does it say?'

McKay took in a breath. He wiped his lips and sank another gulp of Coke.

'So, you decided to open the envelope. Bravo! I knew your curiosity would get the better of you. There is a sign at the cross paths in Crongton Park. It points to where the lido is, the children's play area, the bowling green, the duck pond, the

toilets and the cafe. The sign is your starting point. Take the year of birth of this civil rights leader and place the decimal point after the first three numbers. Mark down the number of steps. This national hero came before Martin Luther King and Malcolm X. He's not American. You won't find him in any text at school – they don't teach you about him. Head due north-west. There you will find. M.'

'Anyone understood that?' I asked. 'My hard drive's stopped whirring.'

'It's a civil rights leader,' Boy from the Hills said. 'We have to work out who it might be.'

'Manjaro's playing a game,' said McKay. 'He's gonna have you running around in circles, squares and triangles for nothing. He's probably laughing out his guts right now.'

'Why would he do that?' I replied. 'A man like Manjaro? You really think he's gonna take the time to plan some *Mission Impossible* treasure hunt while he's hiding from the feds, selling his dragon-hip shit and warring with the North Crong? *No!*'

'You've got a point,' said Boy from the Hills. 'And that black star must mean something. It's gotta be a clue?'

McKay dropped the black star on the pool table.

I picked it up.

'Manjaro wears a black star ring,' I revealed.

We all glanced at each other. Playing pool was forgotten.

'If we're gonna go on this mission,' McKay said. 'Liccle Bit has to be told.'

'If the starting point is the cross paths,' Boy from the

In The Ends

Hills said. 'He must've buried something nearby. It's pure grass, bush and mud around there.'

'Manjaro spilled that when he was a liccle yout,' I said, 'his fave book was *Treasure Island*. His pops used to read it to him.'

'Don't they hunt for treasure in that story?' asked Boy from the Hills.

'They sure do.' I nodded. 'My sis read it once. Long John Silver, hidden treasure chests, yo-ho-ho and boats full of gold.'

'Anybody got a spade?' McKay asked. 'And a compass? More importantly, can anybody read a friggin compass?'

'You bruvs are forgetting something,' I cut in. 'It says on the note we should walk north-west, right?'

McKay and Boy from the Hills re-read the instructions. They both nodded.

'Head due north-west,' McKay repeated.

'What's wrong with that?' Boy from the Hills wanted to know.

'That's North Crong prime estate,' I said. 'Do you think we can just skip into their postcodes and start digging for treasure? North Crong kerbmen are bound to see us.'

'Not if we do it at night,' said Boy from the Hills.

'That's even worse,' I said. 'Night-time is when all the off-key and well-strange peeps roll out to the kerbs and parks. They get their freak on. What do you think they're gonna do when they see our South Crong hands digging for treasure?'

'So, what are we gonna do?' asked McKay. 'Bring a dirty big spade and poke mud in the middle of the day when everyone can sight us?'

'You got a point there,' said Boy from the Hills. 'It has to be at owl o'clock.'

'What time is owl o'clock?' I asked.

'Half one to half two,' replied McKay.

'Are we gonna tell Liccle Bit?' Boy from the Hills wanted to know. He searched our eyes.

'We're not sure if this is for real,' I said. 'If we find someting, we'll let him know.'

McKay and Boy from the Hills both gave a thumbs up.

I took another sip from my drink. *How am I gonna sneak out of my flat at half one in the morning?*

'When are we gonna press go on this mission?' I asked.

'Tomorrow night,' suggested McKay. '*Don't* come with any hi-vis garms. Wear someting dark.'

'Anybody gonna give me another game?' Boy from the Hills asked.

'Yeah,' McKay replied. 'You were well lucky you beat me in the last one.'

'Yeah, right,' Boy from the Hills laughed.

'Hold up, hold up,' I said. 'We still don't know who this civil rights leader is. How are we gonna find that out?'

'Google's your friend,' said McKay. 'Everyone tickle on Google tonight and do your homework. Someting has to come up. When it does, we keep that shit to ourselves . . . for now. Agreed?'

'Agreed!' we all said together.

'Shall we make copies of the letter?' Boy from the Hills wondered. 'Jonah might lose the original. I've got a safe I can keep them in.'

'No,' I replied. 'Keep it to just one. Don't fret – I won't use it as batty paper.'

'Promise?' asked McKay.

'Promise,' I repeated.

'There could be a swag-load of notes,' Boy from the Hills said. 'Can you imagine it? I'll buy a speedboat with my share.'

'I'll get my parents a mansion like this,' I dreamed. 'It might sort out their issues.'

'I'll build a castle and put a restaurant in the middle of it,' said McKay. 'I'll roast kebabs on silver arrows and barbecue ribs on a gold grill. I'll charge twenty notes a pop to Crongton Broadway folk.'

'Do you really think Manjaro's stash could buy all those tings?' I asked.

Everyone thought about it.

'It could all be sweet diddly nothing,' said McKay.

Boy from the Hills set the balls up as I lifted the cue from the table. I played the first shot, but my mind wasn't really on the game. Maybe if there was a bag of money at the end of this mission, my fam could start dining out again once or twice a week instead of sinking rice and pilchards.

6

Empty

I arrived home just before half eight. The flat was quiet. No lights were on in the kitchen. Mum and Dad's bedroom door was closed. No sign of Heather.

I warmed up my fish and rice dinner in the microwave. I had almost finished eating when Heather rolled in through the door all slow-like, looking as if she had just read the most boring book in the world. After she took off her jacket and placed her handbag on the kitchen table, she patted me on the back. 'You all right, bruv?' she asked.

'Yeah, I'm cool,' I replied, a little freaked out by her off-key behaviour.

'You sure?' she pressed.

I nodded. 'Double sure.'

'Something I've gotta tell you,' she said.

'Like what?' I looked at her expectantly.

'Dad,' Heather revealed.

'What about Pops?'

Heather took in a long breath. She placed her hand on my shoulder. She angled her head like the way she used to when I was small. 'Dad... Dad has moved out for a while.'

'What?'

'It's just for the time being,' Heather said. 'Our parents just need... space to sort things out.'

'Where's he staying?' I asked.

'In Ashburton with Uncle Levi.'

I closed my eyes. Something churned and flip-flopped in my belly. *Most parents have their issues, but moving out? I remember how Liccle Bit's pops moving out almost mashed up his fam. They have never really recovered. Pops... moving out. Shooting spikes! It's really happening.*

'Do... do you think they'll sort it out?'

Heather thought about it. She gazed at the fridge. There were magnets on it from Cape Town, Majorca and Bournemouth. 'I really don't know. All we can do is give them time and hope for the best.'

'Shall... shall I ding Dad tonight?'

'No,' Heather replied. 'Give *him* a day or two to get his thoughts together. They're both a bit traumatised.'

'How's Mum?' I asked.

'She's... she's dealing with it in her own way. She's putting on a brave face. It'll take time.'

'Shall... shall I go and chat to her?'

Empty

'Not yet,' Heather advised. 'Maybe leave her until the morning. She needs to process and gather her thoughts too.'

We sat there in silence for the next few minutes. No sound came from Mum's room.

'Try not to worry too much,' said Heather. 'I've got to do some prep for a kerb sale we're having in a week's time.'

'Kerb sale for what?' I asked.

'To raise funds for the youth club building.'

'Oh yeah,' I remembered.

'We need to raise at least seventy grand,' Heather said. 'We've barely got ten. Every liccle penny helps I s'pose.'

I nodded. 'I guess so.'

Heather stood up and headed for her room. Before she got there, she turned around. She looked at me for a long second before she spoke again. 'There's a . . . lot of stuff going on,' she said. 'Trod carefully out there.'

'I will, sis,' I replied, wondering what she knew.

I washed up my plate and made for my room. I didn't bother switching on my TV cos my mind blitzed with a thousand things. I gazed at my Usain Bolt poster. *Should I leak to the feds? Should I spill to Liccle Bit? Should I burn Manjaro's letter? Should I tell Mr Smallwood that I'm super-stressed about my life right now? Do I dare ask out Saira? What day is it? Thursday. Gotta remember extra running training on Saturday morning. Maybe Smallwood's right. All these issues might be blitzing my times.*

I crashed on my bed and stared at the ceiling.

In The Ends

I must have fallen asleep cos it was 1.40 a.m. when I heard my phone vibrate. It was a message from McKay.

> Booyaka! The civil rights leader is Marcus Mosiah Garvey. He was Jamaican. He was all about Black pride and self-determination. He started a shipping company called the Black Star Line. It's definitely him that Manjaro's going on about. My pops says that old-school reggae artists are always chanting about him. Oh, he wore some funky hats, loved going on parades and was married to a lady called Amy. He was born a zillion years ago – in 1887.

I switched on my bedside lamp and blinked. I clawed the matter out of my eyes. I reached to my rucksack and picked out Manjaro's letter. I re-read it. *Place the decimal point after the first three numbers. 188.7. Head due north-west. Oh my gosh! Is this for real?*

I replied to McKay's text.

> Neat homework, bruv. So, are we pressing go on this mission tomorrow night?

McKay didn't take too long to answer.

> Yep. Boy from the Hills has got a dirty big spade and a compass. He even knows how to use it. And he's got a pair of wellington boots. He's on mud duty! Manjaro's treasure-hunt mission is all go.

Empty

I wondered if I should leak my family issues to McKay. I decided against it. He sounded proper excited. I didn't want to piss on his vibe. *He'll probably find out quick-time anyway. My estate loves to chat about other people's business. Miss Crow from her ground floor flat has probably told everybody in the Crongton universe.*

I replied to McKay's text.

See you at school tomorrow. Remember, keep this on a low profile. Don't even spill to your pillow or your imaginary girlfriend.

Instead of replying to my latest text, McKay dinged me.

'I haven't got an imaginary girlfriend,' he argued.

'Stop lying,' I said. 'Remember you told me about that dream you had?'

'You remember that?'

'Yeah,' I said.

McKay killed the call.

7

School's Out

I woke up sniffing bacon and sausages. I couldn't remember the last time Mum had cooked breakfast. *Maybe my last birthday?* I checked the time: 7.10 a.m. I jumped out of bed, Usain-Bolted to the bathroom, screeched to a halt at the mirror, scrubbed my molars and took a shower. I didn't want to miss out on a fry-up.

By the time I made my way to the kitchen, scrambled eggs, mushrooms, sausages and bacon blessed a lonely plate. A glass of apple juice sat beside it. Mum, wearing her long pink dressing gown, washed up a frying pan in the sink. She sang a hymn.

'*We plough the fields and scatter the good seed on the land.*'

'Morning, Mum,' I greeted her.

'Sit down and eat,' she said. 'Before it gets cold.'

'Thanks, Mum,' I replied. 'Thanks very much.'

I grabbed the brown sauce bottle. I had to tap it a few times to get a dribble out.

'What do you have going on in school today?'

'Er . . . English, maths . . . history in the afternoon.'

I niced up my breakfast with the sauce. Mum turned around. Her eyes looked tired. The crease in her forehead seemed a bit deeper. I noticed flicks of grey kissing her temples. 'Have you been doing your homework?'

'Er . . . yes . . . um, some of it.'

'No matter what's going on in this flat,' Mum said, 'you keep doing what you have to do.'

'I will, Mum,' I replied. 'Are you . . . are you OK?'

Mum smiled from her lips, but it failed to reach her eyes. 'Of course I'm OK,' she said. 'Never better! Now you get that hot breakfast down you and have a good day at school.'

I wanted to chat about Dad but thought better of it. *Mum must've guessed that Heather leaked the breaking news. Perhaps if I wait a bit she might spill more about it. Nah, Mum's not like that. Maybe I'll ding Dad later. See how he is. Uncle Levi's got a one-bedroom flat so Pops must be crashing on the sofa.*

Liccle Bit waited for me at the top of the stairwell. He looked as miserable as a one-armed soggy teddy bear.

'What's up, bruv?' I greeted.

'Venetia's giving me grief,' he replied. He threw his arms in the air like the preacher at Mum's church. 'I texted her eight times last night, telling her I'm sorry and that I'll reach up to her gates next time she invites me.'

'And?'

'And nothing!' Bit raised his voice.

We bounced down the stairs.

'I even said I'd be willing to do work experience with her pops,' Bit added. 'But zero, nish, sweet diddly nothing. I don't know what's wrong with her.'

'She'll cool off,' I said. 'Just don't get dramatic about it all.'

'I'm not getting dramatic,' Bit argued. 'Just want her to answer my texts. I've said I'm sorry. What more does she want?'

McKay had parked himself on the bottom step of our communal stairwell. He read a free local newspaper as he awaited us. 'What's bubbling?' he greeted. 'Everyting sweet?'

Bit shook his head.

'So, Venetia spread a dead worm on your toast?' McKay said to Bit as he threw away the newspaper into a large bin.

'You could say that,' Bit replied. 'More like three worms and a dissected frog.'

'Venetia's not replying to his texts,' I spilled. 'She might be trying to teach you a lesson. It might be a temporary ting.'

'Did you try to ding her?' McKay asked.

'I did,' Bit replied. 'Nuff times. She didn't pick up.'

'This is not good,' McKay said. 'This is not good times three.'

'Don't you think I know that!' Bit shouted, flinging his hands above his head again.

Liccle Bit agonised all the way to school about his relationship with Venetia. In a weird way it was a good thing cos I didn't feel bad about not leaking the breaking news about Manjaro and the treasure hunt. Bit had enough worries in his hard drive.

On my way to my English class, I spotted Venetia and Saira in the hallway. They nodded a quick good morning to me before trotting up the stairs to their lesson.

It was hard to focus on Patrice Lawrence's *Orangeboy* with all the latest drama repeating itself in my head. My English teacher, Ms Blackmon, read out an extract but I wasn't listening. *Should I tell all to Liccle Bit and deal with the fallout? Is this treasure hunt flinging us into the danger zone and should I call it off? Shall I go and see Pops after school? How can I get to chat to Saira on her lonesome so I can pop the question?*

'Jonah Hani!' Ms Blackmon called me out. 'Are you with us today? Can you repeat the paragraph I have just read?'

'Er . . .'

I looked down at my book, but I didn't know a diddly where Ms Blackmon wanted me to start to read from. Taking a clueless guess, I read aloud from where I had dog-eared a page.

Suddenly, there was a shout from the playground. One student stood up and peered out of the window. Another three of my classmates shot up out of their seats and did the same.

'They've got Manjaro!' my history classmate, Juniper, yelled from below. Her hair was purple today.

I stopped reading. Something crunched and twisted in my stomach. Nervous energy fizzed around my brain. *What do they mean, 'they've got Manjaro'? Has he been gored? Shanked? Deleted? He was alive the last time he spoke to me. Oh no – will the feds wanna interview me?!*

I snapped my book shut. Ms Blackmon walked over to the window and the rest of the class followed her. We looked down from our third-floor vantage point.

An adrenaline rush scorched through me.

Who's got Manjaro?

There were ten kids in the playground. Make that twenty. Hold on, forty. Fifty. Kids were pouring out of the school. They foot-slapped to the Wareika Way exit. My fellow students rushed out of class. Chairs screeched. Tables bumped. Ms Blackmon nearly got knocked over in the stampede.

'Come back here this instant!'

No one listened. *Doesn't she understand? They've got Manjaro – the king G of South Crongton.*

Once I spotted McKay, Venetia and Saira scampering in the playground, I put my boosters on and zoomed downstairs.

'They've got Manjaro!'

'Who's got Manjaro?' I wanted to know.

School's Out

By the time I made it to Wareika Way, four fed cars and a van blocked the street. An officer reeled out blue fed tape to cordon off the end of the road and isolate a ground-floor flat. Blue lights flashed. Residents, some still in dressing gowns, watched the show from their balconies. Others stood outside their front doors. A pissed-off dustbin-truck driver stood in front of his vehicle with his arms crossed – his route was blocked. A dog barked from the other end of the street.

'Back into school,' a teacher cried. 'Back into school.'

No one gave a damn.

The feds tried to push us back, but nobody wanted to move. There was movement. Everyone looked to their right. Emerging out of the flat, three officers escorted a handcuffed Manjaro. He put up zero resistance and carried his bald head high. Defiant. He was garmed in a blue shirt, sky-blue tie and blue slacks. Shiny black shoes covered his toes. It was the neatest I had ever seen him. A strange hush settled over the scene. Year 8 kids put their hands over their mouths. Even the teachers had quit ordering us back to school. One of them took the opportunity to puff a cancer stick.

I almost expected a helicopter to be flying above and Sky News anchors poised with fat microphones. The feds checked up and down the street as if an alien was about to burst from a drain.

'He gave himself up,' Morgan Stapleton said.

'He put up no resistance,' someone else commented.

In The Ends

'Who's gonna run tings now in South Crong?'

McKay sidled up to me. 'I never thought I'd see the day,' he whispered into my ear corner. 'Can you believe it? He was hiding out just a few steps from our school.'

'Yeah.' I nodded. 'That's un-crong-believable.'

It didn't make sense. *When Pinchers and Lady P kidnapped me, they drove me a few miles out of the ends.*

Manjaro was storm-trooped to a waiting fed car, its blue light blinking. Before he climbed in, he glanced at me.

Something died in my belly, making a weird noise. I swallowed saliva. *I hope the feds didn't notice that.*

Manjaro winked at me, or at least I thought he did.

He was pushed into the ride.

The passenger door was slammed shut.

'Did you see that?' I asked McKay.

'See what?' McKay asked.

'He winked at me!'

'You're getting paranoid, bruv,' McKay said. 'I didn't see anything.'

Two crusty officers wearing black bullet-proof vests sat either side of Manjaro in the car. It signalled to pull out. Everyone watched its progress as the driver observed the twenty-miles-per-hour speed limit. It didn't seem real. More peeps emerged from their flats. Some school folk were recording all the drama on their phones.

'It's all over,' a teacher yelled. 'Back into school. Right now! The show's over!'

'He can kiss daylight goodbye,' McKay said. 'Bad

porridge and skinny bread's waiting for him.'

'If he gets convicted, he'll get, what?' I asked. 'Fifty years?'

'Sixty,' McKay added. 'He's blessed he's not in America. He'd get three hundred and sixty there.'

'If you don't return to school this instant, there'll be report cards for everyone,' barked a teacher. 'And that includes you, Juniper!'

Juniper was the last student back on school grounds. She grinned as she stomped by the teachers. 'The Manjaro drama is much more exciting than King Henry the womanising Eighth,' she protested. 'It's a historical moment.'

Before I made it back to Ms Blackmon's class, I caught up with Boy from the Hills in a ground-floor corridor.

'Did you see it?' I asked him.

'Yeah,' Boy from the Hills replied. 'The whole school did. Everyone's saying he gave himself up.'

'I think he did,' I said. I pulled Boy from the Hills close to me and tweeted in his ear. 'Pinchers and Lady P weren't with him, and I don't think that was the flat they drove me to. There were steps leading down to a basement. Wareika Way has no houses with basements.'

Boy from the Hills grinned. 'It's like a movie, innit? And we've got a part in it.'

'What? A movie? Should we squash this mission and spill to the feds what we know?'

Boy from the Hills shook his head and started along the hallway. I caught up with him.

'Should we?' I asked again.

'Do you hate living?' he said. 'They'll brand you the snitch king. South Crong kerbmen will put a price on your head. They'll share a pic of your rapid self on their WhatsApp groups – South Crong enemy number one! Snitch kings in Crongton have shorter careers than strippers at a Taliban stag night.'

I didn't think about that. My life in the ends wouldn't be worth breathing.

'Everything's set up neatly for tonight,' Boy from the Hills said. 'If the compass app on my phone doesn't work, I've got my dad's real compass as backup. And there's a spade in my garden shed. In fact, there are two spades so I don't have to be on mud duty on my lonesome.'

Before I could change his mind, Boy from the Hills hot-toed to his lesson.

I was the last to return to my English class. 'Delighted you found your way back.' Ms Blackmon wasn't impressed. 'We were waiting for you. Start from chapter nine if you please, Jonah.'

8

Bad Tidings

I couldn't find my bredrens following my last lesson of the day. I called them but no response. Usually Bit and McKay would wait for me at the school gates. Not today. Although maths did run ten minutes over. Bit hadn't wanted to chat too much at lunch, so I guessed he trod home on his lonesome. Maybe he was triggered to the core about the Manjaro drama and wanted to catch up with Elaine about what went down.

Pops. I searched in my pockets to see if I had the funds to catch a bus and visit him. *Maybe I should ding him first.*

I scrolled down to his number and called him.

The phone rang and rang some more.

I wrote him a message.

Just called to see how you are. Sis told me you're at

Uncle Levi's. Hope you're OK. Let me know when I can see you.

Just as I sent the message, I heard my name being hailed by a female voice.

'Jonah!'

I turned around.

Saira. She walked quickly towards me.

This is promising.

I couldn't kill the grin spreading from my cheeks. *Maybe this is my moment. She might even ask me to link up. That would save me a bag of stress. We'll touch down first at the Cheesecake Lounge and then we'll rattle some toes at the Shenk-I-Sheck club if they let me in.*

She was with Venetia.

Maybe not.

'What's going on?' I greeted. 'Can you believe that Manjaro gave himself up to the feds?'

'Saw the video doing the rounds on social media,' said Saira. 'Feds surrounded the flat and he comes out all calm with his hands up.'

'*Good!*' said Venetia. 'About fricking time. Hope he gets locked up until world peace is declared.'

'So . . . where are you ladies heading?' I asked, changing the subject. I didn't wanna fret in front of the girls about the Manjaro situation.

'I'm going back to Venetia's,' replied Saira. 'We're gonna hang out . . . chat about stuff.'

Bad Tidings

Damn!

'Just want to let you know that despite the drama with me and Bit,' Venetia said, 'I'm still your sister from another mother.'

'Say that again,' I replied. 'What's the play with you and Bit?'

Venetia and Saira swapped glances.

'We've . . . we're taking a timeout,' Venetia revealed.

'A timeout?' I repeated. 'What do you mean a timeout?'

'Me and Bit did chat this afternoon in the library,' explained Venetia. 'It . . . it wasn't working out. He had issues with me, and I had issues with him.'

'Oh,' I replied. 'Sorry to hear.'

I felt awkward, unsure of what to say.

'Is . . . is he OK?'

Venetia hesitated over her answer. 'He'll . . . he'll be OK. It's a temporary ting. Who knows, we might miss each other and link up again. For me, I just need time to think. At the moment, I'm not sure if I can squeeze a boyfriend into my life.'

I wanted to tell her that Bit wouldn't love this temporary timeout ting, but it wasn't my place.

'Just wanted to tell you,' cut in Saira, 'that we could still do stuff together. Sink cheesecakes at the Lounge, watch Venetia doing her dance thing and we'll definitely chant you on when you're running for the school. We'll even hold a banner and make up a dance.'

'Thanks,' I said. 'That would be so cool. I could do with

some support. My times are dropping. Saira, have you got a minute?'

'Not...not now, Jonah,' she replied. 'We'll chat tomorrow sometime. I think I know what you want to ask me. I just wanna see Venetia home and make sure she's OK.'

Oh no! She thinks she knows what I'm gonna ask her! I'm gonna be friend-zoned for eternity. How does she know? My eyes must've lingered too long on her. Damn.

'OK,' I said, trying to hide the disappointment in my face. 'We'll chat tomorrow. *Don't* forget to ding me. See you later, Venetia...Sorry...you know...about what's happened.'

I turned around and made for home. Maybe I should just forget about asking Saira out. Too much shit is going down. Perhaps wait till tings calm down a bit. Then again, if I wait too long and some bruv starts linking with her, I'll never forgive myself.

I was about to enter my slab when my phone vibrated with a message from Boy from the Hills.

We're at McKay's yard. He's making his saltfish chilli fritters. Set your gears to high speed and reach.

I didn't need to be told twice. McKay's saltfish chilli fritters were the tastiest this side of Crongton. He stirred in chilli, tomatoes, spring onions, thyme and scotch bonnet pepper to the cod.

Bad Tidings

I slapped on McKay's gates eight minutes later.

Liccle Bit opened the door. I didn't expect to see him there, so I hid my surprise. I sniffed the saltfish-fritter aroma floating from McKay's kitchen. The smell was lip-smackingly, tongue-delightingly good. It teased the living ribs outta me.

McKay had his mum's fave apron on and was dancing to some tune on his headphones. He raised a wooden spoon in greeting.

'Jonah! You reach. I only have one question. And I want a positive answer. ARE YOU READY TO SAMPLE?'

'Ready to sample!' I yelled back.

I followed Bit to the kitchen table where Boy from the Hills was writing something on a sheet of paper. I took a closer look. It looked like a map. It wasn't a neat one.

'Due north-west from the cross paths is definitely in the bushes,' Boy from the Hills said.

'Hold on a sec.' I snapped his flow. I turned to Bit. 'You know about . . . you know?'

Bit nodded. 'Yeah, I know all about your mission and how Lady P and Pinchers kidnapped your quick self. I thought with your rapidness you could've hot-toed away.'

'They caught me when I wasn't looking,' I explained.

'Hmmm,' questioned Bit. 'Don't know how you missed Pinchers. He's big enough to block out the sun for a total eclipse.'

'Anyway.' I changed the subject. 'What do you think? Is Manjaro playing us?'

'I think it's real,' Bit replied. 'From what I know of Manjaro, he's not gonna waste his time setting up some fake treasure hunt.'

'Are you in?' I asked Bit.

Bit didn't hesitate. 'I'm in,' he replied. 'It'll be someting to focus on . . . you know. It doesn't seem too dangerous. It's not as if we have to step up to Notre Dame and rob the Hunchbacker's stash house.'

'You're not fretting about stomping on to North Crong territory?' I asked Bit. 'Plus, the fact that all the strange folk in Crongton spill out into the park at vampire o'clock?'

'The weird folk roll in Crongton twenty-four-seven,' replied Bit. 'They're all over the damn place.'

'Do you trust Manjaro?' I wanted to know. 'Remember, he smacked down your gran and wanted to delete you.'

Bit nodded. 'Yeah, I hear that,' he said. 'I know my sis was in touch with him cos he wants to see Jerome. Elaine made him promise that he'll never touch any of our fam again.'

'You sure?' I wanted assurance. 'He crashed into your yard and terrorised your family. He's missing nuff pieces from his jigsaw puzzle. The feds might boot him into a chain gang but he's still got peeps working for him.'

Bit thought about it. 'All I can say is that my sis says I've got zero to fear from him ever again . . . I trust her.'

We all glanced at each other.

'How many notes do you think Manjaro buried?' Boy from the Hills asked. 'What kinda stash are we chatting about?'

Bit squinted. 'Money drops into Manjaro's hands like Russian winter snow. It could be ten grand or even a hundred grand. What's the point hiding say... five hundred? No mega-drama in that.'

As I imagined counting ten thousand pounds, McKay served the first two saltfish fritters to Liccle Bit.

'Bon appétit,' McKay said.

'Thanks, bruv.'

Bit sampled the fritter and licked his lips. By the look on his face as he munched away, it hit the pleasure zone.

'I... I heard about you and Venetia,' I said. 'Taking a timeout? What does that mean exactly? Can you link with another girl while you're taking this timeout?'

Bit stared at the floor. He nibbled his lip. 'We didn't even chat about that,' he replied. 'It was like, tings are not working out for us right now so let's take a break and see if we miss each other kinda ting.'

'When word is leaked that you guys are on a timeout,' Boy from the Hills said, 'another bruv is bound to step up to Venetia and wanna date her... maybe even a girl. She could be sampling the lips of a—'

Bit glared at Boy from the Hills. He angled his eyebrows. Boy from the Hills killed his flow.

'I didn't need to hear that,' said Bit.

McKay presented a plate of two saltfish fritters to Boy

from the Hills. He bit half of one and scorched his tongue. 'Water!' he cried. 'Water!'

McKay quickly poured him a glass of water. You could almost hear the sizzle and see the steam as Boy from the Hills sank it. His tongue looked redder than a red pepper.

'You wanna check the taking-a-timeout contract, bruv,' McKay suggested. 'Make sure you find out what you can and can't do. You don't wanna mess up your love programme with Venetia if you're nibbling another girl's ears for example.'

'Can we boot this subject to the kerb?' Bit raised his voice. 'I'm here to learn about the mission and to take my mind off Venetia.'

'Do you know how to use a spade?' I laughed.

'Just tell me what time we're gonna link in Crongton Park?' Bit asked.

'Rendezvous time is one-forty-five a.m.,' Boy from the Hills announced.

'I'll set my alarm for one-thirty,' I said.

'No, no, no!' Bit said. 'I've heard your alarm. *Don't* set it. It's too loud. It'll wake up the whole slab.'

'Then how am I gonna stay awake?'

'By doing what you usually do and watching porn,' McKay laughed.

'I don't watch porn,' I insisted.

'Yes, you do!' Boy from the Hills argued. 'That time in the boys' changing room after gym—'

'That wasn't me!' I defended myself. 'That was Kiran

Cassidy. He was showing it to the perv folk on his new iPhone.'

'Whatever,' said Bit. 'Just make sure you're on time for the rendezvous.'

'Everyone, synchronise your watches,' Boy from the Hills said. 'We meet at the cross paths at one-forty-five a.m. Don't be late.'

'What are you talking about?' McKay chuckled. 'None of us have a fricking watch to synchronise. We're not freeing hostages or on a mission to parachute from a plane into Afghanistan.'

Boy from the Hills ignored McKay's remark. 'And wear dark garms,' he suggested. 'Camouflage would be better. If you've got them, balaclavas would be awesome.'

'Camouflage?' I repeated. 'Balaclavas? Maybe you want us to roll around in grass and mud too?'

Boy from the Hills thought about it. 'That did cross my mind,' he said. 'We should blend in with the park and the woods.'

'There's hound shit in the park and woods and I'm not blending in with that,' I said.

McKay dished up my saltfish fritters. They were delicious with a big D but after sinking one it did feel like a furnace in my mouth.

I drained two glasses of water.

Before I left McKay's, Boy from the Hills made sure we all remembered the rendezvous time. *'Don't* be late,' he warned, checking all our eyes.

In The Ends

*

Bit and I trod back to our slab just before seven. He still wasn't his usual bouncy self. The love bug had walloped him hard. Or maybe talk of Manjaro had triggered him.

'He's twisted,' Bit said. 'Cadazy. A living danger. But he's a scholar as well and he wants to be a pops to Jerome – a weird combo. I still don't know how my sis ended up having a baby for him. Jerome's too cute though.'

We entered the lift of our block. The doors closed. I sniffed a funky smell coming from a corner. For a short second I remembered the time I was trapped inside when the doors wouldn't open. I had banged the doors till my knucklers cried.

'Say we do find someting,' I said. 'If it was, say, ten grand, what would you spend your share on?'

Bit scratched his chin. 'I'd give most of it to Elaine so she could get herself a flat or someting. She and Jerome could land into her new place, and I could jack her room. One of the reasons why I'm short is cos my space is so damn small.'

'Elaine still waiting for the council to house her?' I asked.

'Yep,' Bit replied. 'They offered her a place in Elmers End, but Elaine said that's way too far into the wilderness. Wild coyotes and Tasmanian devils feed on rattlesnakes out there. Only the short little bumpkin buses go to Elmers End, and they only come once a year. And even when you get to the bus stop, you have to get a horse and wagon to your slab. And the drivers of those country buses look off-key.'

Liccle Bit reached his floor. 'Rendezvous one-forty-five a.m.,' he said. 'Don't be late or Boy from the Hills will clong you with his spade.'

I stepped out of the lift when it reached my floor and headed to my front gates. As I turned my key in my front door, I wondered if I should try to ding Dad again.

The hallway was dark, but the kitchen lights were on. Someone was talking. Make that two. Heather and somebody else. Sitting opposite my sis at our small kitchen table was Bit's sis, Elaine. I couldn't remember her ever visiting my yard. I didn't even know that she and Heather were friends.

'Hi,' I greeted them. 'How's tings?'

Whatever they were chatting about came to a full stop.

'Hi, Jonah,' Elaine said. 'We're just . . . catching up.'

'We haven't seen each other for a while,' said Heather. 'We're . . . thinking of ways of raising funds for the youth club building.'

'I . . . I didn't even know you were . . . friends,' I managed.

'Course we are,' said Heather. 'We grew up in the same slab. Went to the same primary school together. Just that when we left school we went into different directions.'

'How's . . . how's Jerome?' I asked.

'He's teething,' replied Elaine. 'So a bit miserable cos of that but otherwise he's all good.'

'You heard about Manjaro?' I wanted to know.

Awkward silence.

Elaine and Heather swapped glances. There was a cold mug of coffee on the table. Elaine picked it up and sipped from it. She pulled a strand of her hair and twirled it around her finger.

'He's Jerome's dad,' Elaine said. 'So, there's a proper sadness there. It's messed up. When he gets older, how do I explain that one? It's a shame cos Manjaro has a decent-working hard drive in his head. Once upon a time he used to love studying. He talked about teaching history at uni for a career. But he was impatient to get what he wanted... too impatient.'

I nodded. I hoped the dread in my eyes didn't give away the fact that Manjaro had kidnapped my slim self.

'Where's Mum?' I asked.

'Sleeping,' Heather replied. 'She hasn't slept for two nights so let her be.'

'Did she cook?' I asked.

'Lamb chops, rice and veg in cartons in the fridge.' Heather pointed. 'Put it on a plate and fling it in the microwave.'

I warmed up my dinner in silence. Elaine occasionally sipped her dead coffee. Something was going down, but I didn't have a diddly what. *Maybe Elaine's sad about the Manjaro drama and needed support. After all, Manjaro's her ex. By the time he's let out he'll be trodding with a bent back and twiddling white whiskers.*

Bad Tidings

I washed up my plate in the sink, placed it in the rack and started for my bedroom.

'Step careful out there,' Elaine said. 'Especially at night. Keep your radar on. Oh, forgot to ask. How's the running?'

'Er... good,' I lied.

I felt guilty. *I must try to get back on point with my Olympic dream.*

I looked at Heather. She gave me a look that told me she wanted privacy.

As soon as I got to my room, I texted Bit.

Your sis is at my yard. Don't think she's ever been here before. When I landed home, they were chatting about something. But when they scoped me, they shut down.

Two minutes later, I got a reply.

Your sis came to my yard soon after Elaine gave birth to Jerome. They were close when they went to primary school. Don't fret, bruv. They don't know anything.

I stared at my Usain Bolt poster, wondering what he would make of it all. I replied to Bit's text.

You're right, bruv. This whole treasure-hunt ting is licking my scare bones. See you at 1.45 a.m.

9

Cross Paths

I tried to crash for an hour or three, but nervous energy kept me awake. I sneaked out into the hallway at about 11.30 p.m. for a glass of water. The kitchen light was still on. Elaine and Heather were in deep conversation. They sat very close to one another. Their tones were low – almost a whisper. Their eyes looked proper serious. I couldn't pick up anything they said.

I turned back around into my room and played a FIFA football game on my Nintendo to kill time.

11.52 a.m. I heard footsteps. The front door opening. I crept over to my door and eased it open a crack. 'Stay in touch,' I heard Elaine say. 'Let's just keep this on a low profile. I can't even tell my mum cos she would go cadazy to the power of ten.'

'Give a hug to Jerome for me,' replied Heather.

'Will do.'

The front door closed.

Heather's gates shut two minutes later. All was quiet. All was dark.

Jack on a track! I wonder if Elaine's pregnant again?

There was no way I was gonna crash into the land of sleep now, so I pulled on my black jeans and my dark blue sweater. I found a dusty black bobble hat in the corner of my wardrobe. I squeezed on an old black pair of Puma trainers.

I was ready.

Gosh, it's only midnight. Another hour and a half.

I slapped my headphones on, plugged them into my phone and listened to grime tunes.

Tension rapidly grew like Jack's beanstalk inside me. *What if Mum is up and about at 1.30 a.m.? Even worse, Heather might come out of her room just as I'm about to step. What if a North Crong terror squad is waiting for us at the spot where we dig for Manjaro's treasure? Say Heather catches my gone-missing ass when I get back to the flat? This could be proper dangerous to my future health. Why am I doing it?*

I thought about it.

I can't let my bredrens down. Bit looked very up for it. Boy from the Hills is in commando mode and McKay might fry up some more of his chilli saltfish fritters if we have a successful mission. And I can't lie. The money would be useful to the max. Dad could come home. They'd be no more ding-dong arguments inside my yard. If there was any change left I'd nice up my wardrobe and sink a super-duper raspberry cheesecake at least twice a week.

The time went by in super-slow motion.

Finally, 1.29 a.m.

I opened my door and peered into the dark. The hallway was clear. All I could hear was the hum of the fridge, the next-door neighbour's TV and the occasional whoosh of distant traffic. I passed the kitchen. The digital clock on the microwave blinked. I had to remember the floor creaked outside Heather's room. I slow-toed towards the front door. It looked a distance away. I took in short breaths. At any second, I expected a bright light to shine in my face.

Shit.

Forgot to close my door.

I crept back. I shut it as gently as I could.

I avoided the wailing floor tile on my way back out, and carefully opened the front door. I felt the cool air hit my cheeks. My heartbeat decelerated. I pulled my bobble hat on. I wouldn't even have tried this if Dad were here. The lecture would've continued till the next millennium.

I crept to the communal staircase and bombed down the steps as if village folk with pitchforks and spiky clubs hunted me.

Apart from two South Crong kerbmen who smoked rockets and wheelied on their bikes, the byways and pathways of my estate were empty.

I made it into the park. There was a tramp lipping a bottle on one of the benches and a woman in her dressing gown and hairnet who went by chatting to herself. Nobody was in the fields.

I took the central walkway and headed for the cross paths sign. Streetlights were spaced about thirty metres apart, but it was still darker than a demon's heart. The tweeting of the birds in treetops brought a bit of comfort.

Should've taken a torch. Wait a minute – if I have to, I can use the light on my phone.

I stood under the signposts at 1.41 a.m. The streetlight next to it made a strange buzzing sound. Flies flew around it. Spiders had made cobwebs on it.

I heard faraway voices drifting in from the North Crong side of the path. My heartbeat felt like a heavy mallet.

Where is everybody?

'Jonah!'

I almost jumped out of my black skin and joined a lighter race.

It was Boy from the Hills. He was dressed from head to toe in black. A utility belt wrapped his waist. A dark bulky rucksack covered his back.

'Where did you come from?' I asked.

'I've been here since one-thirty-three a.m.,' he replied. 'Just got back from a scouting mission. All is clear. The North Crong enemy are not on patrol. I watched you arrive.'

I looked along the North–South path and spotted McKay and Bit jogging towards us. They both wore dark baseball caps and black hoodies.

Boy from the Hills checked his watch. 'Two minutes to rendezvous,' he said. 'Excellent prompt arrival.'

He knelt, pulled off his rucksack and unzipped it. He took out a compass and a box of surgical gloves. I was sure that if we had to climb a mountain, he'd have gear for that too.

'What's with the surgical gloves?' I asked. 'You're not gonna have a wank in the woods, are you?'

'*No!*' He raised his voice as Bit and McKay joined us. 'We wear 'em so our fingerprints are not on anything. Everybody, put on your gloves,' Boy from the Hills ordered. 'Precautions.'

We did what we were told.

'Right,' said Boy from the Hills. He pointed the way with his compass. 'One hundred and eighty-eight steps . . . or is it one hundred and eighty-nine?'

We peered north-west to the woods. They looked as dark and intimidating as a tangled forest in a slasher movie. *Wait a second. In those kinda films there's usually only one survivor. Everybody else gets chopped, diced and minced.* I imagined bloodthirsty bats, two-headed birds and red-eyed wolves. Boy from the Hills led the way. 'Do you realise this is North Crong territory?' I mentioned. 'Just saying.'

'They're not gonna defend mud and trees,' Bit replied.

We entered the wood. The ground was still soft and muddy from two-day-old rainfall. The birdsong no longer soothed my nerves – I wanted them to shut the frick up.

Boy from the Hills took out a torch. He sipped from a bottle of water. *Man! He's prepped to the max.*

'I'll count,' said Boy from the Hills.

We trod close together in single file.

After a while, McKay asked. 'How many steps?'

'A hundred and three,' replied Boy from the Hills.

We marched deeper into the wood. There were shallow hollows where autumn leaves had collected. I couldn't see the sky. Owls and other creatures made their night-time sounds. The rush of occasional traffic seemed very far away.

'This is proper ridiculous,' I said. 'Manjaro's having a laugh. He's probably buried a chest-full of shit.'

Boy from the Hills raised his right arm. He stopped and shone his torch at a tree. 'We've got about fifty steps to go,' he said. 'My guess is that tree marks the spot.'

There was a short rise we had to climb before we dipped into a low valley. Shallow puddles stained my trainers. The tree that Boy from the Hills had indicated had the thickest trunk of any of its neighbours.

'What's that?' McKay said.

'What's what?' I replied.

McKay pointed. 'Shine there,' he instructed.

Boy from the Hills did what he was told. 'It's . . . it's a black star.'

'The black star!' I repeated. 'No jokes? We're in the right place!'

'God is good,' said Bit.

'Yep, he or she sure is.' Boy from the Hills nodded.

'Someone's painted a black star about head height.'

'There's something below it,' I said. 'Let's hope it leads to the stash.'

Boy from the Hills dipped his torch.

We could all see a black arrow pointing towards the ground. We stared at each other. Something flapped and chirped above but we didn't pay it any mind.

'How many steps have we trod?' McKay asked.

'A hundred and eighty-eight.'

'Shit on a buttercup,' Bit said. 'Let's dig.'

Boy from the Hills took out two short shovels from his rucksack. He handed me one. We cleared the leaves and twigs that had gathered just in front of the tree. He shone the torch on the ground, which looked as if it had been disturbed. A darker, moist soil mingled with drier earth. Insects that I couldn't name hurried and scurried here and there. Boy from the Hills was careful not to excavate too close to the roots.

I can't lie. My heart boomed. I felt the vibration in my throat. *Ten grand! A hundred grand! Might be able to send my parents on a holiday back to South Africa. They could go shark-spotting – something my dad used to do when he was a kid.*

I stamped down hard on the shoulder of the shovel. I dug deep and removed the earth. Boy from the Hills did the same. McKay held the torch as Bit looked on.

Thirty centimetres deep.

Apart from a dead worm and what looked like the

remains of a beetle, there was nothing.

'Keep going,' McKay urged. 'Deeper. Put some energy into it.'

'Why don't you take a turn?' I said to him.

'Cos I'm holding the torch,' McKay replied.

Half a metre deep.

There was something.

Boy from the Hills struck it first.

It sounded metallic.

I threw down my spade and cleared the mud and debris away with my hands. I ripped my surgical gloves.

It was a black metal box. About thirty centimetres square. Twenty centimetres deep. It had a gold handle fixed to the top. Boy from the Hills helped me pull it out.

'Oh my nights,' said McKay. 'This shit is for real.'

I could almost feel the plane tickets in my hand.

There was a key inserted into a side of the container. It was a cashbox. The torchlight reflected brightly off it.

'What are you waiting for?' Bit pressed. 'Open it!'

Boy from the Hills placed it gently on the ground. He took out an antibacterial cloth from his backpack and wiped it. We looked at it in wonder. He turned the key. It made a clicking sound. McKay shone the torchlight just centimetres away. My heartbeat went into overdrive. I pulled off my bobble hat cos sweat was itching my forehead.

Boy from the Hills opened the cashbox.

A small model ship painted in black. A scroll was

In The Ends

Blu-Tacked to a matchstick-sized mast. Someone had left a handwritten message. I picked up the ship, peeled off the Blu Tack and examined the note. The words were neat and tiny. My bredrens spotted what lay at the bottom of the cashbox before I did.

A withered white flower lay on top of a see-through polythene bag.

'It's a lily,' said Boy from the Hills. 'A very dead lily.'

'Don't fling it away,' warned McKay. 'It might be a clue.'

The polythene bag contained bank notes. Lots of them. The top one was twenty pounds.

My eyes widened. I couldn't help but think of brand-new running spikes and the widest flat-screen TV for my bedroom.

'How . . . how much do you reckon is there?' Bit asked.

'At least a grand,' replied Boy from the Hills.

'Oh my nights!' yelled McKay. 'We can feast at the Cheesecake Lounge every day. Or even upgrade to that posho bistro on Crongton Broadway. They do this duck dish that's the bomb.'

'I'm gonna have to get a bigger wallet,' said Bit.

'You eat duck?' I wanted to know. 'That's gross!'

'You don't know what you're missing,' McKay replied.

A noise.

A rustle in the bushes.

A muffled sound.

Maybe a fox. Or a grizzly bear. Don't be cadazy, Jonah. This is Crongton, not Beartown, USA.

Then, something snapped.

Did someone step on a twig? McKay flashed his torch beyond the wide tree.

'Who is it?' McKay asked. 'Who's over there? Stop frigging about!'

Footsteps? Someone running away?

We side-eyed each other.

'I'm not waiting to find out what that is,' I said.

I placed the ship in the cashbox and picked up my shovel. Boy from the Hills slapped the box shut and locked it. He held it under his armpit and grabbed his spade. He checked our eyes. 'Time to abort,' he said. 'Run!'

I didn't need to be told twice. Usain Bolt would've been proud of me. I torpedoed past our rendezvous point and didn't stop until I reached the tall slabs on Linval Thompson Way.

Bit, McKay and Boy from the Hills just about managed to keep up with me.

We rested at the foot of a tower block. McKay panted the hardest. He could've made a hot drink with the sweat pouring off his forehead.

'Someone was there!' I said. 'I definitely heard footsteps.'

'It might've been a fox or a rabbit,' replied Boy from the Hills.

'Or a cat,' suggested Bit.

McKay shook his head. 'I'm not too sure,' he said. 'When foxes run, they don't sound like *that*. It was human feet.'

'Or wolf paws,' I fretted.

'You're getting paranoid,' said Boy from the Hills. 'Remember, at night, sounds are amplified.'

'I hope you're not wrong,' I said. 'It sounded like a Bigfoot to me.'

'You got the cashbox?' Bit asked.

Boy from the Hills held it aloft. 'I didn't drop it.'

'What time does your pops finish his shift?' I asked McKay.

'Six a.m.,' he replied.

'Let's rendezvous there now,' suggested Boy from the Hills. 'I wanna read that rolled-up note.'

'Can't we wait till morning?' I suggested. 'If Heather catches my slim self out of the door at this time of night, she'll slap me back into my childhood.'

'You're not mousing out now, Jonah,' Bit growled at me. 'Boy from the Hills said we're gonna rendezvous at McKay's yard. And that's what we're gonna do.'

'OK,' I agreed. 'Don't bust a blood vessel.'

We made our way through the alleyways and pathways to McKay's slab. The lift reeked of a giant goblin's fart.

'We're walking up the steps,' said Boy from the Hills.

'What?' replied McKay. 'After that run I can barely put one toe in front of the other.'

'Stop squealing,' I said. 'Best to use the stairs so nobody sees us in the lift at this time of night.'

McKay nodded.

Nine minutes later, we parked around McKay's kitchen table. Boy from the Hills opened the cashbox and carefully placed the dead white lily on the table. McKay poured us apple juice. I picked up the scroll, rolled it out flat and read aloud.

Nuff respect due!

You made it to the big oak tree on the North Crongton side.

I used to dare my crew to tread there and back in the middle of a hot day.

It was part of the initiation process.

I wanted to see who would mouse out with the North Crong watching.

The big question is:

Do you want to double your money?

Or even quadruple it?

Who's got the heart of a proper South Crongtonian?

Do you really, really want this?

Who's gonna mouse out on this mission?

Please turn over.

I flipped the scroll over.

If you want to continue the search for the jackpot, find the author of these words:

'Life springs from death; and from the graves of patriot men and women spring living nations.'

The author's book rests in the North Crong Library in the non-fiction section.

Find it.
Non-fiction is a big section of the library.
You're gonna have to do your homework on this one.
The white lily is a clue.

'North Crong Library!' I repeated. 'Isn't that close to the outside basketball court?'

Bit nodded. 'It's opposite.'

'Then it's end of mission,' I said. 'There's no fricking way I'm gonna step up to North Crong gangster central.'

'Didn't you read the note?' Boy from the Hills cut in. 'We could quadruple our money.'

'Weren't you there when we got kidnapped by Festus and his crew?' I asked. 'Weren't you there in the garage? I don't know about you, but it freaked the bogey outta me. If it wasn't for McKay's older bruv, we could've been bare bones and skulls in a forensic lab. The jury would've scoped pics of us with bullet holes in our heads. We're lucky to be breathing today.'

'It's not like that,' Bit argued.

'North Crong is *all* like that,' I snapped. 'The most dangerous ends in the world. Ruled by the king kerb-rat himself, Major Worries. The Gs walk with pet crocodiles. Grannies wear steel-capped boots. Cuddly animal toys wear bulletproof vests. Even peeps on Universal Credit get jacked.'

'I think you're over-hyping it,' said Bit.

'By the way,' said McKay. 'Who's got the dollars?'

Boy from the Hills unzipped a section of his utility belt. He took out the wad of notes.

'Count it!' ordered Bit.

Boy from the Hills pulled off his surgical gloves and squeezed on a new pair. He checked our eyes and counted the cash.

'Two grand,' said Boy from the Hills. 'Two fricking *grand*. Can you believe it?'

The cash covered McKay's round kitchen table.

No one said anything for the next twenty seconds. If my maths was right, if Manjaro quadrupled the money, there'd be eight grand in the jackpot.

Maybe North Crong is not as dangerous after all.

'How are we gonna get into North Crong Library?' McKay asked.

'I can't go in there,' said Bit. 'Them gully folk know my face.'

'They know my face too,' I added.

'And they definitely know mine,' said McKay. 'And my name.'

'They might not remember my features,' said Boy from the Hills. 'I'll go in.'

'Wait a sec,' I cut in. 'We don't even know what we're looking for. Read the note again.'

Boy from the Hills picked up the scroll. He read very slowly. '"Life springs from death; and from the graves of patriot men and women spring living nations."'

'Martin Luther King,' I guessed.

'Malcolm X?' suggested McKay.

'We're definitely gonna have to smack Google again,' said Bit.

Boy from the Hills stared at the table. He closed his eyes and reopened them. 'I've got an idea,' he said. 'It's bonkers, but it might work.'

'What's that?' I asked. 'For us to t'ief an aeroplane, fly it and parachute on top of North Crong Library?'

'The girls,' said Boy from the Hills.

'What girls?' I asked.

'Venetia and Saira,' replied Boy from the Hills.

Liccle Bit stood up and shook his head. 'In the history of the world, that's the worst idea anyone has ever had since the T. rexes refused to step on Noah's Ark.'

'Festus and his crew know what Venetia and Saira look like too,' cut in McKay. 'Remember, Venetia gored him with a nail file.'

An icy chill raced through my veins as my mind brought up the image of Festus's face. I thought his eyes were about to pop.

'Just listen up,' said Boy from the Hills. 'Who's gonna bring more attention? Two girls stepping into North Crong Library or the three of us? I mean, how many bruvs we know actually step into South Crong Library?'

'I can't even remember where South Crong Library is,' Bit admitted. 'Is it near the South Crong Fitness Lounge?'

'That's my point,' said Boy from the Hills. 'Three bruvs rolling into North Crong Library looks proper suspicious.

All eyes will be on them. It's a different situation for two girls. It'll be normal.'

Bit sat down. 'He does have a point,' he said. 'But Venetia will never go for it. Since what happened to her cousin, she doesn't want anything to do with kerbman business.'

'But this is different,' said Boy from the Hills. 'We're not hiding a gun or doing anything to help a G. We're actually taking *from* them. It's a Robin vibe.'

'Don't ask me to step up to Venetia and tell her about our new mission,' Bit said. 'We're hardly chatting anyway. We're on a timeout, remember.'

'I'll do it,' I offered. 'I'm gonna chat with Saira tomorrow anyway.'

'Hold on to your hounds!' McKay cut me off. 'Don't spill zero to Venetia or Saira until we know who wrote those words. What is it again?'

'"Life springs from death; and from the graves of patriot men and women spring living nations,"' Boy from the Hills repeated. 'I'll share it on our WhatsApp group. *Don't* send it to anyone else. In fact, once you learn it, delete that shit. Come to think of it, we need to burn all of Manjaro's notes.'

We nodded in agreement.

'I wanna keep the liccle black ship though.' McKay grinned. 'That'll nice up my window sill.'

'Stop lying,' Bit chuckled. 'You wanna play with it in the bath.'

We all laughed at that one.

'If there isn't any more mission info, I'm gonna step home and land in my bed before my sis or my mum finds out I'm not there,' I said. 'It's two-forty. If they catch me being outside at mad o'clock, you won't see me till I graduate.'

'Understood,' said Boy from the Hills. 'When everyone reaches home, start on the homework. After that, we'll work out a way for at least one of us to get into North Crong Library and fetch the book.'

10

Saira's Confession

I managed to land in my room safely. Just as I changed into my jammies, my phone vibrated.

It was a text from Boy from the Hills.

> The author of that speech is some Irish bruv called Patrick Pearse. He was a key member of the Irish Nationalists. The British government terminated his ass in 1916. He got blazed by a firing squad. The white lily was a symbol of his movement. He wrote a book called 16Lives. That must be the one in North Crong Library. Manjaro might be the king of kerb-rats, but he knows his shit.

I couldn't forget that following our kidnap by psycho Festus and his crew, my pops made me swear that I'd never trod on North Crong turf again. It was the longest lecture he had ever given me. *'Do you understand that I'm trying to protect you, Jonah?'* he'd said. *'I know you think I'm too strict and I'm stopping you going out with your friends. It's my job to keep you safe.'* Dad's line repeated in my head for untold days. I swore never to land my toes on North Crongton turf again. Mum and Heather heard my promise too.

What to do! What to do? If I press the green button on this one, my fam might never speak to me again. They could call the social services to take me away to some mad place. But there's up to eight Gs on offer. What's the maths on that? Between six of us that'll be around £1,300 each! I'm on this. It'll help out Mum and Dad. I might even donate some big-boy change to Heather's youth-club-building fund. Give them a hundred pounds or something.

I replied to Boy from the Hills' text.

Good work, bruv. When are we gonna step to North Crong Library?

Boy from the Hills replied immediately.

Maybe after school on Monday. Depends what the girls say when you drop this mission on them. We'll have to get out of our uniform before we plant a toe in Major Worries' kingdom.

I only slept for about an hour that night. I tried to boot Festus and the kidnapping out of my mind but couldn't do it. North Crongton triggered the spooks outta me. I wondered if my friends suffered the same way. I messaged Bit.

> Are you sure about stepping back to North Crong? Especially where the library is located? There are more Gs chilling out there than in ten Scrabble packs. We'll be like wildebeest skipping up to peckish lions.

Bit didn't respond for half an hour.

> I'm good with it. Don't think too many North Crong rodents are gonna spend time scoping the entrance of the library.

Rain smacked my window the next morning.

I was the last one to arrive at Crongton Heath Rec. Year 9 and 10 athletes, including Donald Ottey and Merlene Quarrie, stretched and sprinted in short bursts to warm up. Grey clouds kissed the treetops. Drizzle licked the air. I could just about place one toe in front of the other. My stomach growled cos I didn't have enough time to sink any brekkie. I should've sunk a coffee or something first.

Mr Smallwood looked at me with his arms folded and shook his head.

'Right, team,' Smallwood said. 'We're gonna jog up to Falcon Ridge.'

'Falcon Ridge!' I repeated. 'That's like a million feet above sea-level. Only falcons and bird-folk belong there. They didn't call it Human Ridge for a reason.'

Smallwood grinned. 'It'll build your stamina.'

I glanced up at the Crongton equivalent of Mount Everest. I could barely see it through the mist. I imagined arctic blizzards, shivering Inuits and broad-toed Yetis.

Donald, Merlene and the others weren't looking too ecstatic about it either.

Smallwood led the way along a wet, wriggly mud-path that cut through oak and pine trees. I nearly slipped over twice cos of the underfoot conditions. We passed a fenced-off Scouts complex and crossed a mountain bike track.

Old folk said wolves and wild hounds trod these parts, but today they'd been wise enough to stay in their dens.

My thighs and calves hollered for mercy, but Smallwood kept going. I thought of Godzilla roasting him with his breath and spreading him in a sandwich for a hot snack.

'Jonah!' he roared. 'Keep up!'

I wasn't sure how I dragged myself up to Falcon Ridge. Needless to say, I was the last one to reach the summit.

The breeze blows fierce up here.

I wobbled on weak legs towards the viewing platform. I couldn't lie – the view over Crongton and the surrounding area was magnificent. Peering through the clouds, I could make out the ends of Monks Orchard, Biggin Spires and Shrublands. I dropped my hands to my knees and puffed like an old-school choo-choo train.

Smallwood stepped up to me. The wind messed up whatever hair he still had. 'Well done, Jonah,' he said. 'This will be good for your lungs.'

'It doesn't feel like it,' I replied.

'Does it hurt?' Smallwood asked.

I nodded.

'Good!' Smallwood said. 'You want to win, right? The regional champs are in three weeks' time.'

'Yeah,' I said. 'Of course I wanna win.'

Smallwood smiled again. 'Winning costs,' he said. 'And this is where you start paying. We'll do the same again this time next week.'

'Don't they have scheduled flights up here?' I joked. 'Falcon Airways?'

No one laughed, but I caught Smallwood grinning. He was a hard-knock coach, but I vowed from this point to give my best. The regional champs were coming up quick-time and I wanted to show the Crongton universe what I could do.

We rested for ten minutes before we slow-toed back to Crongton Heath Rec. By the time we reached there, the rain had quit.

Waiting outside the changing rooms was Saira. I straightened my posture. She looked so much prettier out of her school uniform, in her blue jeans, black ankle boots and a beige wraparound cardigan. Dark mascara niced up her eyes. A gold stud sexed up her nose. Her black hair was twisted into braids – Venetia probably did it for her. She smiled and waved at me as I passed.

Maybe this is the moment. Why would she trek to Crongton Heath Rec just to see me? She could've dinged me and linked me in Crong Park. Yeah, she's on me. Don't mess it up, Jonah. Ask her about her week. Be cool. Don't stare!

I showered quick-time and wished I'd brought my deodorant. I prayed that no Falcon Ridge whiff lingered on my lean ass. I fixed my hair the best I could and picked the matter out of my eyes.

Ready.

Saira drained a bottle of water when I came outside. She smiled again when she spotted me.

'Tha . . . thanks for coming out here to link up,' I said.

'I wanted to catch you running,' she said. 'You had already gone when I reached.'

'It wasn't pretty,' I replied. 'Smallwood took us up to Falcon Ridge. He's in beret-hat commando mode. I think next time he'll have us carrying backpacks full of rocks up there. There's an asylum ward named after him somewhere in the world.'

Saira laughed out loud.

A good start, Jonah. Don't frig it up!

We walked and talked.

'How was your week?' I asked.

'A bit dramatic,' Saira replied. 'On Wednesday, Mum got a letter from an uncle in Syria that said someone had spotted my dad. We were up half the night chatting about it, so I forgot to do my history homework. Thursday morning, Mr James munched a chunk outta my ear cos I didn't do the Battle of the Somme thing.'

'The Somme thing?' I repeated. 'Basically, it's all about faraway generals ordering army folk to delete each other over a whole heap of mud.'

Saira half smiled.

'And it's good, isn't it?' I added. 'That an uncle saw your pops.'

'Heard it before,' Saira said. She shrugged. 'I can't count how many times someone has seen Pops. But nothing happens. The trail goes dead. He disappears. I don't wanna get my hopes up.'

'Yeah, best not to,' I offered.

'Then teachers had a go at me cos I forgot to do homework or whatever,' she went on.

'Rough,' I said. 'Teachers just don't get it when we're under stress.'

'No, they don't,' she agreed. 'And on top of that, Bit and Venetia had their timeout issues. I had to support her on that.'

'I hear you,' I said.

'And, finally, our boiler's having issues,' Saira went on. 'I haven't had a hot shower for four days!'

'You can . . . er . . . If you like you can use mine.'

Jonah! What are you saying? Don't mess it up!

I closed my eyes, thinking that Saira would boot me into team perv.

'Thanks for the offer,' she said. 'But it's all right – I just boil the kettle, pour it into a bowl with cold water and have a strip wash. It's just inconvenient.'

I did all I could to rid the image of a naked Saira from my mind.

I failed.

'Do . . . do you think Bit and Venetia will ever get back together?'

Saira thought about it. 'Not sure,' she replied. 'Venetia's well busy these days with her dancing and drama club. And her pops is always giving her grief about boyfriends.'

I took in a breath. 'What about you?' I asked. 'Would your family give you grief if you had a boyfriend?'

We rolled on for another thirty metres before Saira replied. 'I don't think my mum would mind,' she said. 'Dad . . . if he were around, he might drop two words about it. He's a bit like Venetia's pops really.'

This is my chance! Ask her, Jonah. Don't mouse it.

'Would . . . would you consider, you know, going somewhere with me, like, I dunno . . . the Crongton Superbowl? Or take in a film at the Crong Max? Or we could sample the new deluxe raspberry ripple cheesecake at the Lounge?'

Saira smiled. *Gosh, she looks so cute when she does that.*

'Jonah,' she started. 'I like you a lot, but—'

'But what?' I cut in.

I hate buts!

Saira breathed in a big one. *What has she got to be nervous about?*

'I . . . I'm trying to work out who I am,' she said. 'Who . . . who I like.'

'What do you mean?' I wanted to know. 'You like me . . . don't you? We have a connection . . . don't we?'

She stopped walking. She pulled my arm so I faced her. She picked out a spot of mud from my hair and smiled again.

'My sexuality,' she said. 'I'm attracted to boys . . . and girls . . . I think.'

I didn't realise it at first, but my mouth opened. I wasn't sure how to respond. I shifted my weight to the other foot. 'Er . . .' I managed.

'So . . . until I work it out,' she stuttered, 'I'm gonna wait to start dating. I've . . . I've had a few offers.'

'Oh . . . right,' I said.

I wondered who had hit on her.

Something right-hooked my heart. My ego took an uppercut too. *Don't show how hurt you are, Jonah. Be mega-mature about all this.*

'You're still my friend?' Saira asked.

I gazed into her eyes and didn't know how that was possible. I needed a moment to suck in my disappointment.

'Jonah?' She wanted an answer.

'Course,' I finally replied. 'Crongton Knights one and all.'

'Thanks, Jonah.'

Saira hugged me hard. It felt good. I couldn't lie – I imagined smacking tongues with her.

'It means a lot to me that we're still mates,' she said. 'Just be patient with me.'

'I'll try,' I chuckled.

'Maybe . . . maybe I might have to accept that I'm bi,' she admitted.

'Bi?' I repeated. 'Bi? Tri? Fry? I don't mind, as long as you end up liking me.'

She laughed again and punched me playfully on my chest.

We trod on for another forty metres. My leg muscles ached but I tried not to show it.

'So . . . does Venetia tickle your fancy buttons?' I asked.

Saira giggled again. It took her a few seconds to compose herself. *You're making her laugh. That's good, Jonah.*

'Just cos I admitted I'm attracted to girls, it doesn't mean that I go for anything in a skirt,' she said.

'Oh, er, sorry about that.'

'Venetia's very pretty,' she added. 'And she's my best friend.'

'Yeah, course she is.' I nodded.

'So, what have you guys been up to lately?' she wanted to know.

I was well glad she changed the subject.

'Have you got time to step to the park?' I asked.

'Yeah,' she replied. 'Mum wants me to help her with the shopping later though.'

Twenty minutes later, we dropped on a bench in Crongton Park. We sat about five hundred metres away from the cross paths sign. My mind relived the excavation of Manjaro's black ship.

Saira's Confession

I was about to start to tell her about it, but I hesitated. A skinny jogger sped by.

'What is it, Jonah?' Saira pushed. 'You've gone all ghost on me. Unlock your tongue, bruv.'

I took in a breath. 'We're on a mission and we need you and Venetia to help us out.'

'I'm listening.'

I told the full story from when I'd been kidnapped by Lady P and Pinchers till the reading of Manjaro's note at McKay's flat.

'Eight grand!' Saira raised her voice. Her eyebrows kissed her fringe. 'Is anybody else hunting for Manjaro's treasure?'

'I... I'm not sure,' I replied. 'I still think someone was night-stepping about in the woods when we dug up the black ship. Are you gonna help? You think Venetia will be on it? You know what she's like about kerbman activity.'

Saira thought about it. 'Yeah, I'm on it.' She nodded. 'Gs like Manjaro do so much negative shit in our community, so why can't we take their funds? If the feds find the treasure, they're not gonna give it back to the community, are they?'

'No, they won't,' I agreed. 'They'll spend it on a name-brand submarine or something or make more road ramps. You think Venetia will be up for it?'

'I can't promise she will,' Saira replied. 'We're linking later today after I've done the shopping.'

'Will you ding me to confirm?' I asked.

'Course,' Saira replied. 'And, er... thanks for understanding. It means a lot.'

She gave me another hug. I wanted to kiss her again.

Jonah, you're gonna have to be patient till she's ready to make a decision. Deal with it.

'What are you doing for the rest of the day?' Saira asked.

'Gonna see my pops,' I replied.

'See your dad? Isn't he at home?'

'No... he's... he moved out for a bit.'

Oh my days, I'm telling her my personal stuff. First time I've spilled to a girl. I might as well roll with it. 'My parents are having a timeout too.'

'Sorry, Jonah. Didn't know.'

'Pops has had trouble getting work since he was made redundant,' I explained. 'Hard-time pressure has licked our yard. My pockets are about as empty as an MP's promise. Mum and Dad are clashing more and more.'

'I hear you.' Saira nodded. 'Hope they get back together quick-time and I'm praying your pops will find another job.'

'That's why this mission is so important,' I said. 'Any piece of the treasure I get can help pay our bills.'

'I hear you again,' she said.

'And that'll make it easier for Pops to come back,' I added.

She squeezed my shoulder. 'Tings will get better. Trust me on that.'

'Thanks, Saira,' I replied. 'I hope they will.'

'I've got to roll back and go shopping with Mum,' Saira said. 'Then I'll see Venetia and see what she's saying. I'll chime you later.'

'OK, thanks for that, and thanks and praises for coming out to the rec to link with me. Appreciate it. And for listening to my home drama.'

'Home drama,' Saira repeated. 'You don't wanna get me started on that one. I've got five seasons to spill.'

11

Smoothing Walls

Mum still hadn't leaked anything to me about Dad moving out. I hoped it was just a temporary thing where my parents had to cool down a dose before they started chatting to each other again.

I couldn't remember the last time I trekked up to Ashburton. It might've been when I was in Year 4. My mum had dragged me along to Ashburton market and bought me a cheapo pair of plimsolls for gym.

The bus took long. I peered out from the top deck towards Fireclaw Heath as we crawled towards the grimy ends of South Ashburton.

You didn't see as many young people on their bikes, scooters and skateboards as you did in South Crong. Ashburton High Street was full of cheap chicken takeaways, kebab shops, pound stores, hair and nail salons, Greggs outlets and convenience stores selling international phone cards. The street-food market was a bustle but traders trying to sell bargain garms had a tough time.

Uncle Levi lived just off the market above a dry cleaner. His flat was never cold. Dad said he was taking me out for a surprise trip. I thought of the funfair that had opened on Biggin Spires Common, but then I remembered Dad's money issues. *Gosh, it's a long time since I had some big fun.*

I pressed the buzzer at Uncle Levi's. Dad opened the front door and led me up to the first-floor flat. I noticed spots of grey on his unshaven chin. His eyes were half closed.

I parked myself in an armchair and took in my surroundings. A portrait of Steve Biko hung from one wall. A framed photo of Miriam Makeba smiled opposite. A selection of African masks and books filled the two other walls. *Maybe if I become an Olympic champion one day, Uncle Levi will have a pic of me blessing his space.*

I sniffed the aroma of an incense stick. 'Where's Uncle Levi?' I asked.

'He's out seeing his girlfriend for the day,' Dad replied. 'He's been working hard all week.'

'What about your week?' I asked.

Dad went to the small kitchen where he took out a bottle of beer for himself. 'Do you want anything?' he asked. 'There are some cans of Coke here.'

'I'll have one, please.'

He gave me a can of Coke. He opened his bottle, took a generous glug and wiped his lips with the back of his hand before he sat down next to me.

'Not really slept,' he finally replied. 'Just trying to make myself useful.'

'How?' I asked.

'By helping out Levi with his painting and decorating,' he explained. 'In fact, do you wanna earn some pocket money this afternoon?'

'Doing what?' I asked.

'By helping me strip some walls,' Dad said. 'Gonna make a start on it today rather than Monday. I've got the keys to the place.'

I caught Dad's eyes. 'This . . . you . . . living here with Levi. It's just temporary, right?'

Dad stood up. For two minutes he was very still. Tears filled the corners of his eyes. He stared out of the window and sank more beer. He didn't turn around to face me when he finally spoke. 'I've gotta be honest with you . . . I don't know if I'll be coming back, Jonah. Not to live anyway.'

'What do you mean?' I asked. 'Aren't . . . aren't you just having money worries?'

His chin dropped to his collarbone. 'Yes,' he replied. 'We're definitely having money worries. But there's more to it than that.'

'Like what?' I wanted to know.

He turned around and gazed at me for a few seconds.

I'd never seen him look so vulnerable. 'It's hard to explain,' he said. 'Drifting, I guess.'

'Drifting?' I repeated.

'Yes.' Dad nodded. 'Maybe it's that. We still love each other but . . . it's not the same. Not like when we first met. We fell in love, did crazy stuff. When your mother said yes to my proposal, I sang all the way home, waking up all the people in our small village. We got married, had Heather and you . . .' Dad's voice faded to a whisper. 'We've . . . we've grown apart.' He wiped a tear from his cheek. He looked out of the window once more. 'We don't really share the same . . . interests.

'I guess me being made redundant made us both think about . . . things,' he continued. 'When you're working all the hours you can, you tend to put home life aside. The two of us were just too busy.'

'I get it, Dad,' I said. 'Right now, you're on the down-low. In your race, you stepped in a puddle and fell over a hurdle. But with time you'll bounce back up, get a job and you'll be back on the track . . . back home.'

Dad didn't respond.

This is serious times ten.

The banter of the market below suddenly rang loud to me. Something emptied from my chest. A tingly sensation filled me.

'I'll do my very best to make sure you'll be OK,' Dad promised. 'I'll have something to give to your mum at the end of the week and I've got a few job interviews lined up.'

'Maybe . . . maybe you need a break with Mum,' I suggested. 'Go away somewhere. Just you and her.'

Dad shook his head. 'Even if I did have the money for that, I'm not sure it's a good idea.'

'You have to try,' I urged. 'It can't . . . can't be the end.'

Dad grimaced. He was about to say something, but he stopped himself. He stared at his feet.

'The truth is,' he finally said, 'that maybe we only stayed together for this long because we had you and Heather to look after and the bills to pay.'

'You still have us to look after,' I replied.

Dad didn't reply. Instead, he parked himself beside me, put an arm around my shoulders and finished his beer.

I did my best to stop myself from bawling.

Dad drove Levi's car. It had a built-in satnav. We headed to an address in West Ashburton. Range Rovers and other four-wheel drives niced up the driveways. The avenue was broad, and the hedges were neatly shaved. Flowers sexed up bay windows. A neighbourhood-watch camera was fixed high on a lamppost. Once inside the house, I was given a big bucket, a sponge and a metal scraper.

Dad led me to this enormous front room where there was enough space for an elephant to chill with a family-size bag of snacks.

'Peel the wallpaper,' ordered Dad.

I was given a stepladder.

I did what I was told. Dad worked on the wall opposite

to mine. A small digital radio played R&B in the corner of the room but all I could think of was that Dad wasn't rolling back home.

It was hard work.

After two hours of stripping and shredding, my palms had developed blisters. My fingers throbbed. Muscles in my right arm ached. Dad examined my hands. He grinned. 'They're not used to hard work,' he said.

'I'll drive you back to Crongton,' he offered.

He pulled a twenty-pound note out of his trouser pocket and presented it to me. 'For people like us, money doesn't come easy,' he said. 'You have to work for it. There's no cutting corners. I don't want you to end up like those boys who take shortcuts. You know who I'm talking about? Those guys who hang on street corners selling their . . . stuff.'

I nodded.

I thought about the hunt for Manjaro's treasure and swallowed a gallon of guilt. *What would Dad say if I offered him funds to help pay the bills? He'll probably reject it. I hope he sinks his pride cos it might help him and Mum get back on track.*

'Spend it wisely,' Dad advised. 'Or save it.'

Pops dropped me off on Crongton High Street. He admitted he didn't really want to face Mum until he had some funds to give her.

So a big ting of this cussing match is money.

I started for home when my phone buzzed.

It was Boy from the Hills.

'We're at Barrington's Hollywood Diner,' he said. 'We're munching sweet potato fries and sinking strawberry and chocolate smoothies. McKay, Bit, Saira, Venetia are all here, and you'll never guess who else?'

'Who?' I wondered.

'Juniper.'

'Juniper!' I repeated. 'She's in my history class. I've noticed that she's been flexing with Saira and Venetia recently. Why's she mingling with you guys?'

'All will be revealed when you set your rapid feet to Olympic mode and reach,' Boy from the Hills replied. 'Sweet potato fries with a dose of mayonnaise is the lick by the way. You have to try it.'

'By the way,' I said. 'How's Venetia and Bit getting on?'

'Kinda weird,' replied Boy from the Hills. 'They're chatting to everyone else but not to each other. They're gonna have to deal with their situation cos we have a serious mission to plan.'

12

Barrington's Hollywood Diner

There were a lot more black and Asian actors blessing the walls of the diner than the last time I sank a smoothie there. Among others there were Bruce Lee, Eddie Murphy, Michelle Yeoh, Jamie Foxx, Angela Bassett, Jackie Chan, Chadwick Boseman and my personal fave, Lupita Nyong'o.

I approached the counter and ordered sweet potato fries and a raspberry smoothie. I took out my twenty-pound note. I felt sweet cos I didn't have to sweat about how I was gonna pay for it.

My friends were parked in the far corner. Bit and Venetia sat at opposite ends. Glasses and plates covered their table. Juniper rocked grey and black fatigues with a US army cap. Black Dr. Martens boots, which almost reached up to her knees, wrapped her toes.

I joined my crew.

'So, how's your pops?' Bit asked.

I shrugged. 'OK, I think. He's doing a bit of work – painting and decorating.'

'When's he coming back?' Saira wanted to know.

'I'm . . . I'm not sure,' I said. 'Can . . . can we change the subject?'

'We're just sorry to hear about their issues,' Venetia added. 'Hope they get back together soon.'

'Thanks,' I said.

'Yeah, I'm praying they sort out their issues too,' added Bit.

Venetia and Bit side-eyed each other. I could taste a dose of awkwardness.

I sat down, blessed my sweet potato fries with mayonnaise and sampled it. Boy from the Hills wasn't lying – my taste buds partied as if it was Chinese New Year.

I looked up at Juniper. She sank her own banana smoothie. 'Have you come to offer us discounts at your pop's store?' I asked. 'The price of a Twirl bar there is scandal-rageous.'

Juniper shook her head. 'Nope,' she replied.

'Then why are you here?' I wanted to know.

Everyone glanced at each other.

Finally, Venetia spoke. 'Cos she's gonna help us out,' she explained.

'Help us out?' I repeated. I checked McKay's and Bit's eyes.

'You have to pass the open-air basketball court to get to North Crong Library,' said Bit. 'Festus and his crew know all of our faces. We can't ask Saira and Venetia to roll up there.'

'Hold your hounds!' I cut in. I looked at Venetia. 'Are you on this? You don't love kerbman business.'

Venetia leaned towards me. 'You're not wrong,' she said. 'I hate Gs and gulley rats. But, yeah, I'm on it. In a rush. Otherwise, I wouldn't be here. Let Manjaro pay!'

'He's paying in jail time,' I said.

'Whatever funds I get from this mission,' Venetia cut me off, 'I'm gonna slap it into a bereavement fund for families who've lost their sons, daughters, cousins and anyone else to gang violence.'

'And that's where my pennies are going too,' Saira added.

Guilt smacked me upside my head for wanting a pair of Puma spikes. *Maybe I should give all of it to my parents.*

'So, who's gonna step up to the library?' I wanted to know.

'Best for someone to bounce up there that they don't know,' McKay replied.

'Juniper!' I guessed.

'You know it makes sense.' Saira nodded. 'They don't know her.'

'She's still a foreign face in hostile ends,' I argued.

I looked at Juniper. Her grin was as wide as the street where I stripped a wall. *Does she understand the pot of shit she's jumping into?*

'And where are we gonna be?' I asked. 'We can't just let her bounce up there on her lonesome.'

'We'll be close by,' said Boy from the Hills. 'Don't fret – we'll have her on radar.'

I stared at Juniper once again. She side-eyed me. 'So, you know everything?' I asked her.

'Yep,' she replied. 'Can't work out that you have the most rapid toes in our year, and you let yourself get kidnapped by Pinchers and Lady P? How did that tragedy happen?'

'They took me by surprise,' I replied. 'I wasn't looking their way.'

'Anyway,' Juniper said. 'Venetia thought it made sense to rope me into your mission. And it's a big one.'

'It's mega,' I said. 'We're talking North Crong kerb-rat central. We're talking Major Worries, the emperor of the North. Have you ever been up them sides?'

'Nope,' Juniper replied. 'Have you?'

'Er . . .'

Embarrassment slapped my cheeks.

'Manjaro and his crew always stepped into my store,' Juniper said. 'Sometimes late at night. He was forever buying up bars of chocolate, ice lollies and cigarette papers. He had a thing for Polo mints and interior design mags too. His crew bought untold bottles of tonic wine.'

'He won't get any of those things doing a long stretch,' McKay said. 'Maybe with his danger rating, he'll get a sweet job in the prison library. The screws will give him what he wants.'

'Never seemed dangerous to me,' Juniper said. 'He'd always pay with a twenty-pound note, sometimes a fifty, and he'd tell me to keep the change. My pops always gave him the proper change back, but I never did.'

'We're not dealing with Manjaro any more,' Bit cut in. 'As I said, we're talking about Major Worries' kingdom. This is *not* a game of water bombs in the park.'

'They don't know me,' Juniper said. 'And if I'm on this mission I want an equal share. Let me drop that one in there before the game starts.'

We exchanged glances. I sank a few sweet potato fries and hunted it down with my raspberry smoothie.

'It's the best option,' said Venetia. 'Equal share works for me.'

Saira nodded. Bit and McKay scoped me.

'We're with the girls,' McKay said. 'It's the safest way we can get that damn book outta the library. What's it called again?'

'*16Lives*,' Boy from the Hills replied. 'I reckon Manjaro left the next clue in there.'

'By Patrick Pearse,' Juniper added. 'You can trust me on this.'

I leaned towards Juniper and trapped her in my gaze. 'Swear on it!' I pressed.

'Swear on what?' Juniper asked.

'Swear that you won't leak to any living soul including your pops,' I demanded.

'You serious?' Juniper asked.

'Serious like a Russian general playing chess. Hold your hand up.'

Juniper raised her right palm. 'OK, I swear that I'll never spill to anyone who's not at this table anything to do with the North Crong Library mission.'

Everyone nodded.

'Satisfied?' Bit asked me.

'I'm good,' I said. 'What's the plan?'

Boy from the Hills took out a folded-up piece of A3 paper and spread it out on the table. He brought up a map of North Crongton on his phone, and then he sketched a map of the roads and pathways leading up to North Crong Library.

'There's a kids' play area here.' He indicated. 'We can chill on the benches, watch the kids on the swings, and still have a view of the library. It's not too close to the basketball court.'

'What time?' Bit asked.

'The library closes at six,' replied Boy from the Hills. 'ETA at the kids' play area is five-thirty p.m.'

'Stop chatting in commando tones!' snapped Saira. 'What's ETA?'

'Estimated time of arrival,' Boy from the Hills said. 'Make sure you change out of your uniform before you step up to North Crong. *Don't* wear anything blue. Not even nail varnish, socks or a blue biro in your pocket.'

'We're not stupid,' said Venetia.

'Shall we link up at the Crongton roundabout?' Bit

asked. 'My pops lives near to there. If we need to hot-step it from the kids' play area, we can make my pops' place our safety base.'

'Can he cook?' asked McKay. 'Might need food if the North Crong infidel siege our South Crong asses. Has he got any lamb shanks? Baby potatoes? Asparagus?'

'Lamb shanks?' repeated Bit. 'Aspara-what? You're always thinking of your belly.'

'Guilty,' admitted McKay. 'But you never answered my question: can your pops cook?'

'Yes, he can cook if you have to know.' Bit raised his voice.

'Is that a wrap?' I asked. I looked at Boy from the Hills. 'Or is this the time you hand out our AK47s and grenades?'

Saira and McKay laughed but Venetia folded her arms and gave me a brutal eye-pass. *'Don't* joke about guns,' she said. 'You know I don't love that.'

Juniper shook her head. 'Even I know not to chat about guns when Venetia's around.'

'Sorry,' I offered.

Embarrassed, I munched my sweet potato fries in quick-time.

'To confirm,' said Boy from the Hills, 'ETA is *five-thirty p.m*. None of you get detention on Monday.'

We all glared at Juniper.

'Why are you scoping me?' she protested.

'Cos you get detention eight days a week,' said Venetia.

'There are only five days of school in a week,' argued Juniper.

'But you get my drift.' Venetia smiled. 'Quit insulting the teachers and behave your rude self on Monday.'

'I don't know about you,' replied Juniper. 'But there's a coffee-caramel-flavoured smoothie with my name on it.'

'Gross!' yelled McKay. 'They should be outlawed!'

Juniper didn't care. She marched up to the counter and ordered her smoothie.

13

Heavyweight Knock-Out

I reached home just after six-thirty p.m. Mum had cooked fried chicken wings, pasta and broccoli. As I munched my dinner, she didn't say much. She just sipped her hot chocolate and smiled at me. Before she went to her room, she placed her palm on my cheek and said, 'Be good, Jonah.'

'Good night, Mum.'

I heard Mum switch on the radio. She listened to music from a gospel station. I guessed it gave her comfort.

I didn't see her for the rest of the night.

I watched an ancient Disney film, *The Sword in the Stone*, to take my mind off all my worries and stresses. I laughed out loud for the first time in a while as Merlin tried to imitate a bird.

Heather rolled in just before eight. She parked herself

beside me and spoke in a whisper. 'How's Dad?'

'He's OK,' I replied. 'He's got himself a little part-time job helping out Uncle Levi.'

'That's good,' said Heather. 'Hopefully, Uncle Levi can give him more work and Pops can get back on his feet – maybe come home soon.'

I didn't respond.

'Is he eating well?' Heather asked.

'I think so.'

'How did he look?'

'Unshaven. Tired.'

'Things will be all right,' Heather insisted. 'It'll all work out.'

She gripped my shoulder. 'Didn't I tell you?' she added.

I gazed at the TV screen. Merlin cast a spell to perform the washing-up in the kitchen.

'Jonah?'

I turned to Heather. My lips wobbled before I spoke. 'I . . . I don't think Pops is coming home . . . not to live anyway.'

'He said that?' Heather wanted confirmation.

'Er . . . yeah.'

'You sure?'

'My ears aren't twisted, Heather. I heard what I heard from Pops' own mouth.'

'So . . . it's deeper than money issues?' Heather asked.

I looked at my sister. 'There might be a few more issues,' I said. 'But money is numero uno. Dad said he can't even step to our yard without giving some change to Mum. Trust me, if Pops can slap down a bag of dollars on our kitchen table, most of our worries are over.'

She crossed her arms and stared at the TV. Merlin had magicked himself into a rocket and zoomed to Bermuda.

I took out a ten-pound note from my pocket and offered it to her. 'Dad gave me a twenty for peeling a wall,' I said. 'Treated myself down Barrington's Diner but the tenner is to go towards the shopping.'

Heather looked at me as if I had a ginormous slug stepping out of my nose. Slowly, her face curved into a smile. Then she did something she hadn't done for the longest time: she kissed me on the forehead. 'You have a good heart, Jonah.'

For the rest of its running time, we watched the movie in silence. No chuckle was raised. I wondered if Heather had the same gut ache and pain in the brain that I had.

I decided to go to bed early.

I looked up to my Usain Bolt poster. 'I don't suppose your coach allowed you to sink a raspberry smoothie and sweet potato fries with a dose of mayonnaise on them,' I said.

Mr Bolt didn't reply.

I got comfy and didn't bother to change into my bed clothes.

My phone buzzed at 11.50 p.m. I switched on my lamp.

It was an Instagram message from Saira. An image was

attached to it. **You'd better sit your slim self down when you see this.**

She doesn't usually send me pics of herself. She's not into that take-a-selfie-every-other-second-of-the-day thing.

I opened the message. It wasn't a Saira selfie. It was a scene from a car accident. *Pain in the lane!* It appeared that two cars had rammed another from the rear and the side. The driver's door had an oval-shaped dent in it. The front-left headlight was mangled. The registration plate sat at a strange angle. Glass covered the road. I could just make out dark skid marks arching towards the kerb. A blue baseball cap sat upside down on the pavement. Lying on his back, a crusty bald man was sprawled over the tarmac in the star position. He wore a blue T-shirt. It looked as if blood oozed from his left ear. His eyes were open. He was very dead.

The message under the photo said, **Pinchers deleted on the Crong Circular near Palace Road.**

Suddenly, my insides froze over, as if a polar bear had just given me mouth-to-mouth resuscitation. *Pinchers. Dead.* I thought of slapping on Heather's door but changed my mind. *Pinchers. Dead. Is this for real?*

My fingers tingled. I texted Saira. I could hardly type out the words. I pressed untold typos before I got it right.

Can't believe it! I'm stepping over there to check the scene out. Palace Road ends? That's the east side?

Saira didn't take long to send me a reply.

Wait till morning. It was a definite gangland hit. The feds will be there, and you don't know who's gonna be scoping the situation. Best to keep your bony ass indoors.

I didn't know why, but I had to get proper confirmation. I wanted to see for myself. *Pinchers. Dead. It can't be.*

Saira, I have to step. I don't want no second-hand info. I just chatted to that bruv the other day. And now he's in the dead zone. It's creeping the halloweens outta me.

I pulled on my trainers and soft-footed out of the flat. I thought about smacking on Bit's gates but changed my mind. *Bit's mum can get a liccle murderous if you slap on her front door past ten o'clock.*
Saira texted me back.

That bruv kidnapped you the other day.

Once I reached the ground floor, I hot-stepped towards the east ends of South Crongton.

I arrived at Palace Road fourteen minutes later. The feds were there in force. Forensic officers went about their work in white shell suits and blue surgical gloves. They studied something under a bright light. Other officers pitched up a tent. They had already blocked the road with one police van, two cars and blue and white fed tape. A crowd of peeps had assembled, some still wearing their dressing gowns and slippers. They spoke in whispers. A few pointed here and there. Many of them recorded the scene on their phones. Others looked down from tower-block balconies. One guy from the seventh floor watched the drama through a pair of binoculars.

A siren wailed in the distance. There was a cold snap in the air.

'They deleted Pinchers!' someone hollered from above.

'They chopped his neck,' another cried.

'Two cars rammed him,' said somebody else. 'And it looked as if they dragged his crusty ass outta the ride.'

'The blood dripped down the drain when I got here,' a young boy on a scooter said. 'The paramedic didn't take long to brand him dead.'

'The North–South Crong war's gonna go all cruise missile.'

'Nuclear!'

'Good!' said a middle-aged woman, her hair in rollers. 'Let them all kill each other! The rest of us might live in peace. He's not getting any tears from me!'

I closed my eyes. I imagined Pinchers being pulled out of his car and then a North Crong G ripping his throat open with a long, serrated blade. The chill inside refused to quit. I could taste my chicken-wings dinner once again. Suddenly, my legs felt weak. Something roasted inside my brain. I had to sit down.

Heavyweight Knock-Out

I dropped my head into my hands. *Jonah, you're gonna have to drop this Manjaro treasure hunt quick-time. It's getting too fatal. Maybe Pinchers got deleted cos the North Crong are looking for Manjaro's treasure too.*

'Jonah!'

I looked up. It was McKay. I could see his pyjama bottoms poking out above the waistband from his tracksuit trousers. His trainers weren't laced and he wasn't wearing any socks.

'How long have you been here?' McKay asked.

'Just reached,' I replied. 'I think they took the body away.'

'Yep.' McKay nodded. 'I saw the ambulance. Next stop is the morgue. Was just chatting to a bruv. He said they carved his throat so deep you could see the bones and all that tissue and tendon stuff you learn in biology.'

A bloody picture appeared IMAX-size in my inner vision. I shook my head to rid myself of it. I failed.

'The North Crong are getting bold,' said McKay. 'Think about it – they just chopped Pinchers, Manjaro's number one man, on a busy South Crong street.'

'It's brutal times ten,' I agreed. 'There's no more Manjaro to defend the ends.'

'And what's more,' McKay added, 'even if peeps saw it, zero amount are gonna step to the feds to offer themselves as a witness. You know that.'

'Did . . . did Pinchers have family?' I asked.

'Yeah,' replied McKay. 'He must've had. I think Nesta told me one time he has a younger sis.'

'I wonder if they've got Lady P too?'

'If they did, that would be all over social media in a rush,' McKay replied. 'If I were her, I'd stay wherever the freak she is. There must be a bounty on her sweet head. Every apprentice G from North Crong is gonna hunt her down as if she's the Holy Grail.'

'What the frick is the Holy Grail?' I wanted to know. 'It seems as if the North Crong are taking over everywhere.'

'You're not wrong.' McKay nodded.

I felt a tap on my shoulder. I shot up to my feet and spun around.

It was Juniper. Her eyes were wide. 'Someone must've set him up,' Juniper said. 'How did they know that he'd be driving on Palace Road at a particular time? I'm telling you – there's a snitch in Manjaro's crew.'

'It's proper suspicious,' agreed McKay.

'Maybe they're hunting for Manjaro's treasure,' I suggested. 'Don't you think it's kinda strange that days after Manjaro gives himself up to the feds, and after Pinchers kidnaps my ass, Pinchers is dead?'

'Stop getting paranoid.' McKay shook his head. 'It's not as if they tortured him to try to find out where Manjaro left his jackpot.'

'You can't be too sure,' I said. 'For me, the mission is a red-flag ting. It should be stamped with nuff skulls and bones.'

'What?' McKay raised his voice. 'I got up for nothing at owl o'clock to trek to the dark side of the park? To enemy territory beyond the cross paths? And you know that if my brother found out that my ass was out and about in foreign ends, he would go all Terminator on me. And if my pops found out he'd put his forklift truck against my door so I couldn't get out at night.'

'My sis would do the same shit to me,' I said. 'Then my mum and pops would take their turns.'

I peered down Palace Road. The feds had finished erecting the white tent. The bright light stung my eyes. I heard the whoosh of traffic on the Crongton Circular. From a nearby slab, a dog barked from a fourth-floor flat. I spotted a few South Crong kerbmen wearing their puffy blue anoraks and blue baseball caps. They walked around aimlessly. Now and again, they checked their phones. Their usual swagger was missing. They looked defeated.

'Jonah!'

A girl's voice. Saira.

'Are you OK?' she asked.

She wore a baggy baby-blue tracksuit and pink slippers. No make-up marked her face. Her hair looked confused. I smiled a greeting. She was still as pretty as a Bond girl who'd just stepped out of a perfect sea.

'I'm good,' I replied. 'I think. It's a bit of a trauma overload when the bruv who kidnaps your slim bones gets his throat split.'

'I did tell you to keep your curious self indoors,' she said. 'It's gonna be triggering.'

'They why did you hot-foot it over here?'

Saira shrugged. 'Got nosy I suppose. Like everybody else, I wanted to see what was going down. This shit's for real.'

'Jonah's quit the mission,' McKay spilled. 'Said it's too toxic.'

Saira placed her hands on her hips. 'This might not have anything to do with our mission.'

'We don't know that for sure,' I argued. 'Say every G in Crongton is hunting for Manjaro's treasure.'

'If that were true,' Juniper cut in, 'you would've crashed into somebody by now.'

'We have!' I raised my voice. 'There was someone in the woods!'

'It was a fox,' McKay replied. 'Or a fricking gerbil. Who knows? It wasn't a human. We would've seen them.'

'If it were a North Crong G,' added Juniper, 'they're not gonna hot-leg it away from us, are they? We were stamping on North Crong turf. I mean, we're not scary. They would've jacked everything we had.'

'Not even the Year Sevens fear us,' agreed McKay.

'I don't know if I agree,' I said. 'Have you ever been in the same postcode when McKay busts one of his farts? That's triple X-rated shit.'

McKay wasn't amused but the girls chuckled.

I heard a screech of tyres. I looked to my right. Boy from the Hills jumped off his mountain bike. He marched towards us. 'Did you hear?' he panted. 'Did you hear?'

'Hear what?' Juniper replied. 'That Pinchers got rammed by two cars and then had his throat separated from his collarbone? Yep, we heard. Old news.'

'Is he?' Boy from the Hills wanted confirmation. 'Is he . . . ?'

'Deleted?' McKay finished the sentence. 'Yep. In the history of the world, there's never been anyone as soooo dead as Pinchers.'

'The North Crong are taking over,' said Boy from the Hills. 'Soon, we'll be forced to wear black T-shirts, slap on black headscarves, play more b-ball and sell dragon-hip pills to primary school kids. It's grim days ahead.'

'I dunno about you but being so close to where Pinchers got shanked is creeping the bowels outta me,' admitted McKay. 'I'm stepping back to my slab. I need to hook some sleep. I have to get up early to season my turkey thighs and let them marinate.'

'Get up early to season your thighs?' I repeated. 'A bruv, who we all knew, got his windpipe burst and all you can think of is hooking some sleep? That's cold, bredren.'

McKay thought about it. 'That's reality, Jonah,' he replied. 'That's the ends we live in. Name me any year, or even a three-month period, where someone hasn't been gored or shanked in Crongton?'

I couldn't think of an answer.

'It's a regular,' added McKay. 'Like my pops paying his gas bill every three months. You just know that some mum or pops out there is gonna be bawling waterfalls cos their son or daughter has been carved. There are too many tombstone whisperers in Crongton.'

In The Ends

No one spoke for a long minute. McKay wasn't wrong.

Boy from the Hills picked up his bike. The feds reeled out a new tape, fixing it around lampposts. 'Move back!' they ordered the crowd. 'Move back!'

We headed towards our own slabs.

Someone played a drill tune from above. Drizzle licked the air. I pulled my hoodie over my head. Saira's phone chanted a Drake rap. 'It's Bit,' she said.

'Put it on speaker,' Boy from the Hills said.

'What's happening?' asked Bit. 'Can't step outta the flat cos Elaine's up with Jerome.'

'Twitter wasn't wrong,' replied McKay. 'Pinchers got assassinated. It wasn't pretty. His blood dripped down the drain and ghetto rats are probably drinking it up. The ambulance passed me, and it didn't have its sirens blazing. Pinchers is as dead as an old school pharaoh.'

'Was Lady P in the ride?' Bit asked.

'Don't think so,' I said. 'Nobody said she was.'

'If they deleted Pinchers,' Bit said, 'Lady P must be next on Major Worries' list.'

'We might be next on his list!' I raised my voice. 'Don't you get it? This might be over Manjaro's treasure.'

'Nah, bruv,' Bit disagreed. 'Don't think this has got anything to do with it. Mr Paranoid is stroking your brain.'

'That's what I told him,' McKay agreed.

'You don't know that for true,' I argued. 'As far as it goes with me, Manjaro's treasure hunt is over. Finito. Let the credits roll.'

Heavyweight Knock-Out

'What do you mean, "let the credits roll"?' pressed Bit. 'It was you who roped us all in.'

'Yeah,' agreed McKay. 'Because of you, I got my ass up at vampire o'clock to trek to Crong Park. You snapped me out of my dream of being the black Gordon Ramsay.'

'Got two grand out of it, didn't we?' I reminded them. 'Can't we just share that shit and order the raspberry ripple deluxe at the Cheesecake Lounge to celebrate?'

'And forget about the possible eight grand that might be waiting for us at North Crong Library?' Boy from the Hills said.

'Have you lot got a date with Colonel Death?' I asked. 'Didn't you see what happened to Pinchers? Last time I saw him, he was merrily munching Manjaro's spaghetti Bolognese. He sank a beer to hunt it down. Now, anytime soon, he'll be chewing daisies. I don't know about you, but I don't wanna make new bredrens with worms and other mud folk just yet.'

'Nor do we,' said Bit. 'Hold up – my sis is coming. I'll ding you back.'

Saira killed the call.

We rolled on for another block. More peeps passed us on their way to Pinchers' murder scene. Some had already fixed their phones on selfie extensions.

Saira's phone rapped again. She answered it. 'Hold up, Venetia – video-call me back on the Crongton Knights WhatsApp line. I want Bit in on this too.'

Venetia did as she was told. We crowded around Saira's

phone. Bit appeared. He sat on his unmade bed. His bedroom was as small as mine. He could almost touch the walls if he spread his arms. Venetia came into shot in her hallway. She pulled on her black puffy coat. They both looked proper awkward. 'Venetia!' Saira greeted once more. 'Yeah, we're rolling back to our ends now.'

'Major Worries just uploaded something,' Venetia whispered.

'Major Worries what?'

'Major Worries has posted a pic on Instagram,' Venetia said. 'He was shaking his lizard-skin boots at a wedding.'

'A wedding!' I repeated.

'That's classic G behaviour,' said Bit. 'He orders the assassination of Pinchers, and while his gulley rats carry out his command, he's doing the candy dance at some wedding. Standard!'

'He's got himself a serious alibi,' said Saira. 'Has he posted anything else?'

'Not yet,' replied Venetia. 'I'm just stepping out of my slab. I'll link you outside Dagthorn's. Is that OK with you, Juniper?'

'No probs,' Juniper replied. 'Don't expect any freeness from our shop though. My pops is still cussing about me giving away bags of Maltesers and Creme Eggs that had passed their sell-by date.'

Bit shook his head. 'Can't make it,' he said. 'My sis is prowling near the front door. If I go near it, she's gonna proper maul me.'

There was a small bench located in a square just in front of Juniper's store. It was lit by a tall lamppost. Next to it was an overflowing bin. Venetia had already arrived. She wore a black woolly hat and brown leather gloves. She didn't waste time starting the convo.

'We shouldn't quit the mission just because they deleted Pinchers,' Venetia said.

'That's all right for you to say,' I argued. 'They didn't kidnap your bones and freak the shit outta you. I thought I was gonna bring up my brekkie and decorate Manjaro's kitchen with it.'

'I thought Manjaro fed you?' Boy from the Hills said. 'Spaghetti Bolognese, wasn't it?'

'Was the spaghetti Bolognese on point?' McKay wanted to know. 'Did they drain the pasta properly? Or did Manjaro overcook the mince? Did he grate some parmesan cheese over it?'

'McKay!' I raised my voice. 'We're not giving ratings for Manjaro's cooking! You guys might not take this seriously, but a man's throat got proper dissected tonight. And the Gs who did it might be hunting the same jackpot as us. Trust me, my parents could do with a slice of the jackpot but not if I end up munching worms.'

'Nah.' Venetia shook her head. 'North Crong Gs hunting Manjaro's treasure doesn't make sense. If that were true, we'd have seen something by now – some kinda warning. A sign.'

'Didn't you hear those footsteps in the woods?' I

challenged. 'It wasn't a fox, an escaped Kentucky-fried chicken, a big bad wolf or any fricking gerbil!'

'It might've been a ghost,' Juniper offered. 'Yeah, some ghost that lost its way to Fireclaw Heath. I've seen a few of 'em.'

'Are you serious?' asked McKay.

Juniper wasn't smiling. 'Of course I'm serious,' she said. 'Don't you guys believe in ghosts? The afterlife? Things that scrape and howl in the night?'

We all shook our heads.

'Seriously,' said Venetia. 'What's gonna happen if a North Crong G ends up with Manjaro's jackpot?'

'They'll buy a new ride,' replied McKay. 'And new garms. They'll upgrade from shopping in Lidl to Waitrose. If they have any class, they'll sample red wine with their roasted salmon.'

Venetia shook her head. 'Nah, that's not it.'

'Then what's it?' Boy from the Hills wanted to know.

Venetia narrowed her eyes. 'They'll buy more dragon-hip pills to put on the streets,' she replied. 'They'll buy more guns and long shanks to protect themselves. They'll recruit more young peeps to their gangs. Crongton will become even more dangerous.'

'Better those grands in our pockets than any G's.' Saira nodded.

'I . . . I don't know,' I said. 'That kidnapping freaked me out. I don't want that shit to repeat on my slim bones again.'

Heavyweight Knock-Out

Venetia nodded as if she understood my fear. She rubbed her hands together to keep them warm. She looked at me. 'If . . . if you don't wanna step on this mission then that's fine,' she said. 'No shame. But may . . . maybe we'll take it on.'

'What?' I raised my voice. 'Without me? Manjaro gave *me* the letter. It's *my mission*.'

'It's bigger than just your mission,' argued Venetia.

I checked their eyes. 'So . . . are you all thinking the same?'

No one responded.

I dinged Bit and put it on loudspeaker. 'Bit,' I said when he picked up. 'Venetia wants to carry on the mission even if I step out. Are you in or out? Bear in mind that once upon a time, Manjaro terrorised the DNA outta your family. I'm saying we should share the two grand that we have. It's not good to get too grabilicious. What say you, bruv?'

Everything went quiet. All I heard was a tweet from a treetop. I spotted a spider spinning a new home just below the light of the lamppost. McKay wouldn't look at me. Boy from the Hills checked the brakes on his bike. Venetia studied her nails. Saira read something on her phone and Juniper took out this vape smoking thing and puffed from it. Blackcurrant smoke climbed up my nostrils.

'Bit.' I raised my voice. 'Are you still there?'

'Yeah, I'm here,' Bit replied.

'Are you in or out?'

'I'm in, bruv,' Bit replied. 'We started this mission. We might as well get to the end credits.'

'What?' I challenged. 'You sure?'

Silence.

'Are you sure?' I repeated.

'Yeah, I'm sure,' Bit confirmed. 'I'll stay for the ride.'

'This ain't no frickin ride on the big wheel at Spenge-on-Leaf fun fair,' I shouted.

The heat in my head grew intense. I checked my friends' eyes. There was no support there. 'Bit,' I yelled. 'You're just saying go on this mission cos Venetia wants in. She *sacked* your stubby ass but you wanna get back with her. You *know* it's true, bruv. If she said drink the polluted pond water in Crong Park, you would sink gallons of that shit too!'

I murdered the call.

I stared at my friends. McKay shook his head. Boy from the Hills adjusted the light on his back wheel. Saira gazed at her feet. Venetia glared at me as if she wanted to sizzle my tongue on a fiery barbecue.

I'm soooo in the wrong zone. What did I just say? Gotta get outta here.

'That ... that,' I stuttered, 'came out all wrong. Sorry, Venetia. I ... I didn't mean it. You know, not that way.'

Venetia didn't respond.

'I'm ... I'm stepping back to my slab,' I said. 'Sorry, again.'

I walked off in silence.

I glanced over my shoulder once and no one had moved. I didn't think they could believe what I had just spilled.

Jonah, you and your mouth!

I managed to soft-toe back inside my flat without Mum or Heather noticing. I crashed on to my bed and stared at Usain Bolt. 'They're all against me,' I said. 'Can't believe that all my bredrens are thinking about more money when the danger just stepped up a gazillion notches! Though I suppose I could do with my portion of that two grand now. I know it won't bless everything but it'll help to nice up my parents' situation.' Mr Bolt glared back at me as if he was saying he had no answers.

14

The Girl in the White Trench Coat

I didn't sleep too good.
Saira texted me at 1.45 a.m.

Are you OK, Jonah?

I didn't respond.
Bit dinged me at 2 a.m. I refused to pick up.
McKay sent a message at 2.10 a.m.

That wasn't called for, Jonah. Especially the shit about the pond. You must ding Bit and Venetia and apologise again. As if you mean it.

McKay wasn't wrong but I wasn't ready to apologise once more yet. I didn't know what to say.

I got up at 6.45 a.m. The flat was quiet apart from Mum's radio on a low volume in her room. I guessed she had it on for most of the night.

I decided to make my breakfast. Not too many cornflakes were left in the packet. There was barely a dribble of milk remaining. I munched my dry brekkie. I remembered what Mr Smallwood had advised. *You need to build up your stamina, Jonah.*

I hoped all this drama wouldn't affect my running times. *Gonna make an extra effort today.*

I changed into my black Puma tracksuit and pulled on my running trainers.

My slab still slept as I bounced down the staircase. As I landed at ground level, someone switched the streetlights off. It had quit raining, but the pathways and streets were slippery. Puddles rippled at the low end of slopes and around clogged drains.

I jogged past Dagthorn's store. I watched Juniper's pops pull up the shutters and get ready for his day. He smiled at me. I wondered what time Juniper rose in the morning.

Can't imagine why she believes in ghosts.

I hot-footed towards Crongton Heath. When I reached there, the wind bashed against my face.

Four runners lapped around the track. I recognised one of them: Merlene Quarrie. She wore grey tracksuit bottoms and a dark blue hoodie. Her brown locks bounced on her shoulders. I decided to catch her up.

'Merlene!'

She slowed, looked behind and smiled at me.

'Don't usually sight you on a Sunday morning,' she said.

'Smallwood told me I needed to build up my stamina,' I replied. 'I'm fading at the end of my races.'

'He told me the same ting,' she said. 'What's your event?'

'Four hundred metres.'

'That's a killer.' Merlene grinned. She had a nice smile. 'Especially if you race in windy conditions like this. You start off running too fast and by the time you reach three hundred metres, the lactic acid sets in. It's all about pacing yourself.'

We ran side by side. A gold cross dangled from a chain around her neck.

'What's your event?' I asked.

'Eight hundred,' she replied. 'You can sort of ease into it on the first lap but on the last bend it feels like running in thick cornmeal porridge.'

As we completed another four laps, we talked about the upcoming school regional championships.

'You think you got a chance?' Merlene asked me.

I thought about it. 'Not sure,' I replied. 'There's a lot of stuff kicking off in my life right now. To be honest, I haven't really focused. Smallwood's always chatting about being focused.'

'I'm glad I've got the running,' Merlene said. 'It gets me outta the screaming zone in my flat.'

The Girl in the White Trench Coat

'Screaming zone?' I repeated.

'Oh, family tings,' Merlene explained. 'I've got two younger sisters. And a brother from another mother. It'd take me for ever to go through all our issues.'

Out of the corner of my eye, I spotted a young lady in a white trench coat and knee-length black boots. She wore a dark blue beret and quarter-moon-shaped glasses. She watched me from the other side of the long-jump pit. Her hands were in her pockets.

'Who's that?' Merlene asked.

'I'm not sure,' I lied.

'We don't usually get spectators on Crongton Heath on a rainy Sunday morning,' Merlene said. 'She obviously knows you. Are you gonna say hello?'

'She's not my girlfriend or anything,' I insisted.

Merlene threw back her head and laughed. She had neat teeth. 'I worked that one out,' she said. 'She's waaaay too old for you.'

'Nineteen, twenty is not too old for me,' I argued.

'Yes, it most definitely is!' Merlene chuckled. 'Girls usually date a liccle bit older than them, not younger. Especially girls who look like that. Go and see what she wants.'

'I haven't finished my running.'

'Go!' ordered Merlene.

'OK, I'll say a quick hello to her.'

I quit jogging. Merlene flashed me another smile as she picked up speed and hot-toed around a bend. I marched towards the lady in the white trench coat. A gust of wind disturbed the strands of hair that had escaped from her beret. Her collars were up to protect her neck from any further rain. She took her hands out of her coat pockets and adjusted her hat. A lion tattoo growled on her left hand. No lipstick marked her lips. Her once blonde hair with blue highlights was now black. Dark mascara sexed up her eyes.

Lady P.

I wondered what the P stood for.

I took in a breath.

'Tracks on fire!' I said. 'Do . . . do you—'

'Not here,' she warned. 'Follow me.'

She led me on to the path that led to Falcon Ridge.

'You're not taking me up there, are you?' I wondered. 'I've just done four laps.'

'No,' she replied. 'I've seen the view untold times and you can't see anything in this sad weather anyway.'

She pressed on.

She made a sudden turn to her left into woodland. A narrow path wriggled this way and that. Wet tree leaves blocked out the light. Mud stained my trainers.

'Where are you taking me?' I wanted to know.

'Just keep up,' Lady P said.

The bushes were thick, but she seemed to know where she was heading. We climbed a short rise before a green space opened in front of us. It fell away to a little valley of acorn trees. I could see a gravel path ahead and a row of small, terraced houses. A dog barked as we approached a wooden gate. I wondered if Boy from the Hills knew this place.

Lady P lifted the latch and beckoned me along the path that led to a back door. The hound from two houses down quit yapping.

'You live here?'

'Wipe your feet before you step in the house,' she said.

The back garden had solar lamps and little men with fishing rods around a tiny pond. They had bushy white beards. It looked as if someone ancient lived there.

Maybe it's Lady P's gran?

Lady P opened the back door with a long key. I wiped my feet on a bristled brown mat. She hooked her white coat and blue beret on a peg. Her black hair fell to her shoulders. She was incredibly pretty.

The kitchen sink sat below the window that looked out to the back garden. A framed poster of somebody called Pam Grier hung from a wall – she had a mighty Afro. Two smoothie mixers stood on the kitchen counter. Apples, pears, olives and bananas filled a fruit bowl.

'Do you want a cup of tea?' she asked. 'Something hot?'

'No, just water if you have it.'

She opened the fridge and tossed me a bottle of still water.

I drank from it greedily.

'Obviously, you heard,' Lady P said.

'About Pinchers?'

'Yeah, about Pinchers.'

'The whole world knows,' I said. 'When I got to the scene, every fed and their cousin were there. What went down?'

Lady P filled a kettle and switched it to boil. She dropped a bag of green tea into a blue mug. She stared at me as she waited for the kettle to boil.

I'm not sure why, but the nerves inside my belly fizzed, crackled and popped. Yet I simply couldn't leave.

She poured the hot water into her mug and pressed a teaspoon against the tea bag.

'He got grabilicious,' she finally revealed.

'Grabilicious?' I repeated.

'He was driving to meet them,' she said. 'I warned him not to. We had an argument. He shut me down whenever I tried to make a point. He wanted to make a deal, be an equal partner.'

'He was gonna play for the other side?' I asked.

Lady P thought about it. 'Not quite,' she replied. 'The South Crong side is not like it was. Too many defections. And who are left want to wear the crown.'

'Was it Major Worries he wanted to do a deal with?'

'Something like that,' she replied. 'I warned him that Major Worries is the ultimate alpha.'

I sank more water. I wiped my lips with the back of my hand.

Can't believe she's spilling so much to me.

'What's an ultimate alpha?' I wanted to know.

'Someone who doesn't want any equal,' Lady P replied.

'Someone who believes their way is the only way. Someone who will wipe out any challenge to their authority. Someone that is impossible to bargain with. *That's* an ultimate alpha. There's another word for it. Fascism.'

'It sounds . . . sounds as if you know him. Some . . . some peeps say you came from North Crong?'

Lady P didn't answer. Instead, she gazed into her tea.

'What's he like? You know, Major Worries? Have you ever swapped words with him? Is it true he got shanked five times in the chest and survived? Is it true he's killed nuff man?'

'Ask me no question and I can't tell you any lies,' Lady P replied.

'So, you're not gonna spill on that?'

'Nope.'

I finished my water. 'Pinchers' death's got nothing to do with my mission?'

Lady P laughed. She then shook her head. 'Not even I know what was inside your envelope,' she said. 'And Manjaro told me everything . . . well, almost everything. He did chat about trying to leave Jerome something but didn't know how to go about it. Elaine killed his calls.'

'Seriously?' I wanted confirmation.

'I was there nuff times when Manjaro tried to ding her,' Lady P replied. 'He even asked me to call her. I refused. I didn't wanna get involved. Once, when she cut him off, he flung the phone against the wall. I kept out of his way for the rest of that day.'

'Bit's sis doesn't play,' I said.

'No, she doesn't,' Lady P agreed. 'She was one of the very few people who stood up to him. Manjaro was never the same after Elaine left him for good.'

Lady P sipped her tea and looked out to the back garden. 'It's peaceful here,' she said. 'I'd stay here if I could, but life moves on.'

'What are you gonna do?' I asked her.

She looked up to the sky. 'Keep rolling on,' she replied. 'I've got a few things to underline and put a full stop to. Then I'm missing from here.'

'Leave Crongton?'

'Yep, leave Crongton,' she repeated. 'Start afresh. Somewhere far away. Do my degree.'

'What's gonna happen to South Crong?'

Lady P didn't hesitate in her answer. 'Major Worries,' she said. 'That's what's gonna happen to South Crong.'

'Can't anyone stop him?'

Lady P considered it. 'Yeah, there was one we had hope for. He doesn't fear anyone. Peeps would follow him. But I'm not too sure if he wants to bring the fight to the Major.'

'Who's that?' I asked. 'Anyone I know?'

Lady P tasted her tea again. She half smiled. 'You ask a lot of questions,' she said. 'It's best that you don't know.'

'What should I do?' I asked.

Lady P turned around to face me. 'About your mission?'

'Yeah.'

'Manjaro loves to play games,' she replied. 'He's a proper manipulator. He's mischievous with that. He also likes to teach. That I do know.'

'Do you think he'd leave a stash of notes somewhere?' I asked.

Lady P nodded. 'Oh, yes. That sounds like Manjaro. Cash in the right hands can do some good. Notes licking the wrong palms can work their evil. The questions are the same for all of us, including me and you. How much do you want it? What are you prepared to do to get it? And once you get it, how do you make the best use of it?'

'If I had cash blessing my palms I'd put it to good use,' I said. 'You know, help out the fam.'

She finished her tea, dabbed her mouth with a tissue and rolled on lip balm.

'I've finished my last chore for Manjaro,' she said.

'What was that?' I wanted to know.

'He wanted me to gain your trust,' she replied. 'Our first meeting was a bit . . . dramatic. I argued against the bag over your head. He wanted me to tell you and your friends that he's not a cold killer– that he stood up for peeps in the ends.'

'He wanted us to know that?'

Lady P nodded. 'Manjaro's time as the king G is over. He had the sense to put things in place for him when he gets out – I helped him with that. Now, things are gonna get messy in South Crong. Watch your movements.'

'Thanks, I will.'

'You can go now,' she said. 'Think of your next move wisely. Don't stay on the board for too long.'

'If . . . if I want advice, will you be here to give it?'

'Nope,' she replied. 'I'm disappearing. Tomorrow. Gotta keep moving. My time playing this game is done. Whatever you do, treasure your family and friends. That's more important than any stash of notes out there.'

She stared into space as if she remembered some long-ago loss.

'That's what it's all about, really,' she added. 'Good luck.'

'That's it?' I asked.

'Yep, that's it.'

She's not wrong. Family and friends are number one. If Manjaro has left a big stash then I'm gonna make damn sure it's put to the best of use.

15

Apologies

I knew where I had to go.

I made it to Venetia's slab in twenty minutes. I tickled her gates. Her pops answered the door. His shoulders could barely fit in the doorframe. He was dressed in a dark blue suit and a skinny blue tie. He looked me up and down as if I was a bad-mannered trick or treater. I had forgotten I had mud splashes all over me.

'Jonah,' he greeted. 'What brings you here . . . so early? We're about to go to church.'

'Just wanna see Venetia for a sec,' I said. 'I won't take up too much of her time.'

'I hope you're behaving yourself.'

'Yeah, of course.'

He studied my trainers. He wasn't impressed. 'You'd better wait outside,' he said. 'Venetia!'

He left the door ajar, and I breathed a little easier. I imagined how nervous Bit must've been when he dated Venetia.

Wearing a smart black skirt, a beige blouse and a tiny black hat with some kind of netting, Venetia appeared.

My gaze locked on to her hat. It wasn't as cool as Lady P's beret. I tried to kill my chuckle but failed.

'What are you skinning your teeth at?' she snapped.

'Er, nothing . . . nothing.'

'This is my church garms,' she said. 'I *only* wear it when I step to church.'

'That's all good.' I nodded. 'Nothing wrong with church garms. You look . . . very churchlike.'

'Hmmmm.'

'I mean very nice.'

Her face softened.

'You come to say sorry again?'

'Er . . . yeah. I sort of got into my feelings. I didn't mean what I said about the pond and shit.'

Venetia crossed her arms and angled her head. 'I've already let it go,' she said.

'You have?' I asked.

'Yeah, we all know stress is licking you down cos of your parents' situation. It's rough.'

'Yeah, it is. I'm not sure what's gonna happen there.'

'It will play out how it's meant to play out,' Venetia reasoned. 'There's no point them staying together if it makes them unhappy. Trust me, you don't wanna hear that they're staying together *for the kids*. That makes everyone proper miserable.'

I stared at the floor. 'No, I wouldn't want that... Anyway, thought I'd tell you first.'

'Tell me what?'

'I'm in,' I said. 'For the mission.'

Venetia pulled my arm and led me near the lifts. 'What's wrong with you?' she asked in an angry whisper. 'Keep this shit quiet!'

'Sorry.'

'Are you sure?' Venetia wanted confirmation. 'While we're trekking up to North Crong, I don't want you mousing out just before we reach.'

'I won't squeak out,' I said.

'Promise!' she urged.

'I promise,' I said. 'But I'm not gonna lie, when I step on North Crong turf, my heart's gonna be pumping like a cow in the T. rex compound.'

'Mine too.' Venetia nodded. 'It's dangerous in Crongton wherever you step. My cousin, Collette, was minding her own business in South Crong, but look what happened to her.'

'That must still hurt,' I said.

'Yeah, it does,' Venetia said. 'It's coming up to the two-year anniversary since she lost her life in that drive-by shooting. That's why I say let's take their fricking money and put it to good use.'

'And the guy they intended to delete is still trodding the ends?'

'Probably.'

Injustice spread from Venetia's gaze. I wanted to lighten the tone.

'Can't I at least buy a pair of brand-spanking-new Puma spikes?'

Venetia crossed her arms. 'Hmmm.'

'If not the Puma spikes, the super-duper raspberry ripple special at the Cheesecake Lounge?'

Venetia smiled. 'Yeah, I'm sure everyone will be on that.'

'So, this is it,' I said. 'We're really gonna do this.'

'Yep, we are,' Venetia replied.

'What . . . what about your and Bit's situation?' I wanted to know.

Venetia bit her bottom lip. 'We're friends . . . at least I hope we are. Not looking beyond that.'

'OK,' I said. 'I think he's still sweet on you.'

She looked down the hallway. 'I'd better go back inside,' she said. 'Pops doesn't like being late for church.'

'OK, see you tomorrow at school,' I said. 'And don't jack the collection funds.'

'You're full of jokes today,' replied Venetia. *'Don't* mouse out on us tomorrow.'

'I won't.'

16

The North Crongton Library Mission

At school, we had agreed to meet on the green of the Crongton roundabout.

Before I left my slab, I slapped on Bit's gates, but no one answered. I guessed he had left already.

It was quite a trod from my ends, so I jumped on a bus. My destination was the stop outside the kebab shop that stood opposite the green. Roads from there led to Ashburton, Elmers End, North and South Crongton.

The green was about half a football pitch long. The grass in parts grew tall enough for kids to play hide and seek. It stank of piss. Rubbish and plastic bottles piled up on the fringes. A green sofa was abandoned in one corner. It was a strange place to have a basketball hoop and backboard fixed against a graffiti-covered brick slab. North Crong signs and symbols dominated everything else sprayed on the wall. Wild weeds and tufts of grass hid most of the concrete playing space. The whoosh from the traffic wasn't the only thing that chilled me.

I was the second to arrive. Boy from the Hills checked his watch as I approached him. He wore green combat trousers, black trainers, a black hoodie and a backpack. He looked as if he was about to join Sylvester Stallone's *Expendables*.

'You're five minutes early,' he said. 'That's all good. I wish the rest of our crew were as on time.'

Juniper was next to reach. She styled purple dungarees, white trainers and black lipstick. She stepped up to us, bopping her head to whatever was on her headphones.

'This is dramatic, isn't it?' she said. 'Who knows? This could be the last time we see our home ends. North Crong kerbmen might scope us out and say we're spies. They'll bury our South Crong corpses in some forgotten corner of Fireclaw Heath.'

'And good afternoon to you too,' I greeted. *'Don't jinx us.'*

'Just bantering, man,' Juniper said. 'Trying to ease the tension.'

Boy from the Hills peered down the South Crong road. It was full of slow-moving buses and honking taxi drivers. I was surprised he didn't have binoculars. 'There they are,' he said. 'They're stepping together – Saira, Venetia, Bit and McKay.'

'Shit!' Juniper suddenly cursed. She stamped one foot.

'What is it?' I asked.

'I forgot my ginger beer can,' Juniper groaned. 'I left it in the fridge when I got back from school.'

'Is that all you're fretting about?' I asked. 'We're about to step into enemy ends and you're bawling oceans about fricking ginger beer.'

'Some*body* didn't have their Coco Pops this morning.' Juniper grinned.

'Cool off, you two,' Boy from the Hills said. 'Let's not get distracted.'

We were joined by the others.

'Whose idea was it to meet up in this stinkin' place?' complained Venetia. 'We might as well have linked up in a toilet!'

'Not me,' I replied.

'If it's really distressing you,' said Boy from the Hills, 'I've got some armpit breath in my backpack.'

Boy from the Hills pulled out a can of deodorant and showed it to Venetia. Venetia thought about it then shook her head.

'Everyone ready?' Boy from the Hills asked. He searched our eyes.

'Didn't have time to sink my dinner,' replied McKay. 'If this damn book isn't where it's supposed to be, I'm gonna be well vex. But apart from my dinner issues, I'm ripe for this mission.'

'Me too,' added Venetia. 'Just wanna get off this green.'

'And me,' said Saira.

'Do you think they've got any decent fried-chicken takeaway huts?' wondered McKay. 'Bit, once upon a time you roamed the toxic lands of North Crong. Did you sniff anything I might fancy?'

'Finger-licking chicken wasn't on my mind when I trod the foreign ends of North Crong,' said Bit. 'Does your mind think of anything else apart from food?'

McKay thought about it. 'Not really,' he replied.

'Juniper! Juniper!' Boy from the Hills called. 'Where's your backpack? Didn't I ding you to tell you to bring one?'

'Why do I need a backpack?' Juniper asked.

'To put the book in,' Boy from the Hills explained. 'You can't just step out with the book. A librarian will stop you.'

'No problem,' Juniper said. 'I'll just run out with it. They're not gonna bother to chase me.'

'And bring attention to yourself?' I cut in. 'Are you taking this mission serious?'

'If I wasn't taking this shit serious,' said Juniper, 'my ass wouldn't be here!'

'All right! All right!' Boy from the Hills cooled. 'Remember we're on the same team.'

'By the way,' I said. 'What's the plan when we get the book? If we get the book?'

'Rendezvous at my yard, innit,' McKay said. 'If the mood takes me, I might hustle up some roast salmon, mash potato and asparagus.'

'What's asparagus?' Bit wanted to know.

'Rich people's veg,' replied Juniper. 'We don't sell it.'

The North Crongton Library Mission

'What about your pops?' Saira asked McKay. 'Won't he be home?'

'He leaves for work at six,' McKay replied. 'He's still on the zombie shift.'

'OK,' said Boy from the Hills. 'Can we focus on the mission instead of what's on the menu for later? Let's roll.'

'About time,' said Venetia. 'I feel polluted.'

'Gonna take the longest shower when I get home,' said Saira.

We crossed the road.

McKay paused at the kebab shop and licked his lips.

'We haven't got time for that,' Boy from the Hills warned. 'Step it up – we've got twenty-five minutes.'

I couldn't lie, when we landed on the North Crongton Road, something knotted in my stomach. Fear burrowed through my veins.

It was a normal street, with kids performing wheelies on their scooters and bikes. Others kicked footballs against an abandoned car. North Crong gangland art decorated any spare piece of brick, board and concrete. A man dumped a black rubbish bag into a wheelie bin. I couldn't help but think about Pinchers and his split throat.

'What's the name of the book again?' asked Boy from the Hills.

'*16Lives*,' Juniper replied. 'By some guy called Patrick Pearse. Hopefully, it won't take me that long to find.'

Boy from the Hills nodded. 'Good,' he said. 'You know it off by heart.'

I looked ahead.

The road bent left and arched its way around North Crongton. Straight ahead of us were the tall and wide slabs of the estate. I took in a long breath. 'Would be funny if the library was closed today,' I chuckled.

'It's not,' Boy from the Hills said. 'I checked the opening times.'

We stepped through a gap in a low brick wall. We paused for a few seconds to study the estate map. I read the names of the tower blocks – Walter Rodney House, Randolph Turpin House, Aneurin Bevan House, Olive Morris House, Claudia Jones House and Althea Lecointe-Jones House.

I wondered who those peeps were.

Using the map on his phone as a guide, Boy from the Hills led the way.

I sensed North Crongton eyes watching me.

'Can we take a timeout at the shop?' asked McKay. 'I've done over five thousand steps today. I've proper earned my candy.'

'OK,' agreed Boy from the Hills. 'But we can't stay long. The library closes at six.'

Just like back home in South Crong, there was a convenience store in the middle of the estate. It was called Sugar Minott's. A rubbish bin overflowing with drink cans and empty bottles stood on the pavement in front of it. I wondered if Sugar was as grumpy and mean as Juniper's pops.

The North Crongton Library Mission

Parked on a low wall opposite Sugar Minott's were several older teens all dressed in black, topped with dark baseball caps. They munched on their crisps, sank their beers and sucked their vapes and their rockets. They styled black gloves with visible palms.

My heartbeat boomed into fourth gear. 'This might not be a good idea,' I whispered. 'This is North Crong G grand central. If they find out we're from South Crong, we might as well book a meeting with the undertaker.'

I readied myself to hot-toe it outta there.

Venetia side-eyed me.

'Relax,' whispered Boy from the Hills. 'We're just young peeps bouncing about our daily business. No one needs to know what ends we're from.'

We all bought bottles of water, apart from Juniper, who paid for a ginger beer. McKay purchased a Snickers bar and demolished it in four bites. 'Not a proper starter but it filled a hole,' he said.

Fifty metres up the path was a children's play area encircled by a low wooden fence. There were swings, slides, a climbing frame, a seesaw and a mud mound to run up and down.

One lone parent pushed his son on a swing.

We spotted a bench on a small grassy rise that overlooked the play area. We headed for that.

'It's grim up here, man,' said Saira, brushing away the debris from the bench. 'This will be the one and only time I ever visit North Crong. Even the man in the shop looked as if someone shat in his rice pot.'

'Did you see those G men by the shop?' I asked. 'I'm telling you – North Crong has more Gs than America has guns.'

'It was the same when I rolled up here,' said Bit. 'Just try to act normal and ignore them. Don't get in their way. Oh, and *don't* stare.'

'What's normal for North Crong?' wondered McKay.

'Nothing is normal here,' replied Juniper.

'Can we focus?' said Boy from the Hills. He pointed towards a high meshed fence about a hundred metres away. 'On the other side of that fence is the basketball court.'

We peered in the same direction. Six guys played three-a-side football on the Astroturf. They rocked black bandannas and black Nike vest tops.

'On the other side is the library,' said Boy from the Hills. 'You can't see it too good from here.'

'Juniper's gotta step by all that,' I said. 'Isn't there another way to the library?'

'There is,' replied Boy from the Hills. 'But I don't wanna take you down alleyways and paths where we don't know who we might bump into. At least the basketball court is open. A lot of peeps who live in the slabs can see what goes on down there.'

'They're not gonna snitch to the feds that six North Crong kerbmen deleted us,' I said. 'Not even granny folk will spill anything.'

'Can't you take a break from being Mr Negative?' said Venetia.

'Just checking out the dangers,' I replied.

'If we play it casual it'll be cool to step by the basketball court,' said Saira. 'Stop fretting!'

'You hope it'll be cool,' I put in.

'You still wanna do this, Juniper?' asked Venetia.

Juniper shrugged. 'Yeah, why not? If I wasn't here, I'd be outside the back of our shop tearing up cardboard boxes or putting all the plastics in its own bin.'

'You sure?' Boy from the Hills wanted confirmation.

'Are we gonna keep doing this till the library closes?' asked Juniper. 'Let me get on with it.'

Boy from the Hills took out a plastic bag from his backpack. 'Put the book in here,' he said. 'And wrap it up.'

A middle-aged woman went by, clutching her small dog. As it squirmed in her arms, something wriggled in my stomach.

Another two players joined the football match in the basketball court. Three girls, dressed in black jeans, polo-neck sweaters and dark denim jackets, arrived to watch them. One of them used their phone to take a selfie and then a picture of the players.

Someone played Afrobeats from above. I heard a siren in the distance. A white boy with dreadlocks rolled by on his scooter.

'You ready?' Bit asked Juniper.

Juniper nodded.

She folded the plastic bag and held it tight in her right hand. She sucked in a long breath.

'Maybe . . . maybe I should go with her,' offered Bit.

Boy from the Hills shook his head. 'Let's not switch the programme at the last minute.'

We watched her leave.

My heartbeat cannoned into fifth gear.

'Let's at least get a liccle closer,' suggested McKay.

'OK,' agreed Boy from the Hills. 'But not too close. Remember, Festus and his crew know what we look like.'

Juniper marched off as if she was late for registration. We stepped on to the perimeter path that ringed the basketball court. There was another bench outside the forecourt of a slab called Frank Crichlow House. We made for that. My pulse drummed inside my throat. It was as if a gremlin had crawled in there and started to bash my tonsils with a mallet.

Saira, Venetia, McKay and Boy from the Hills squeezed up on the bench. Bit and I stood. I checked this way and that. I felt warm. I unzipped my hoodie.

Banter, curses and shouts floated over from the football game.

'I'm a true baller!' one of them boasted. 'The North Crong Messi.'

'A living shame they stopped the school matches between North and South Crong,' said another.

'True ting,' said the first guy. 'We'd proper whip them.'

'Humiliate them.'

'Destroy them.'

'And jack their dinner money after the game.'

Laughter echoed around the court.

Boy from the Hills stood on the bench. He used his right hand to shield the setting sun from his eyes. 'I can't see Juniper,' he said. 'She must've gone in.'

I checked the time on my phone. 'Five-forty-five,' I said.

'Maybe Bit's right,' said Saira. 'One of us should've gone with her.'

'No one's gonna trouble her,' said Boy from the Hills. 'Nobody knows her here and she's just stepped into the library to get a book. It's an everyday thing. There's no drama.'

'We'll give it two minutes,' Bit said.

'OK,' Boy from the Hills agreed.

The cries from the football game continued. Another siren rang out from the direction of the Crong Circular, or it might have been a sound I heard in my head. A mum emerged from Frank Crichlow house with her little girl. She ranted something about the council not coming out to fix her kitchen sink. Two delivery guys carried cardboard boxes into the slab. We heard a couple having a ding-dong argument in a nearby block.

Five-forty-eight.

I jumped up on the arm of the bench and peered towards the entrance of the library.

No sign of Juniper.

Guilt slapped my conscience. The gremlin whacked my

tonsils some more. Sweat developed in my armpits.

I spotted two of the girls who had been watching the football game stepping towards the library.

'I think we'd better make some strides towards the library,' I said. 'You know, just in case.'

Just as we prepared to leave, a young mixed-race girl, about ten years old, bounced up to us. 'Gotta pound?' she asked. She searched our eyes. 'Or even fifty pence?'

Boy from the Hills had already set off.

Saira checked her purse. She found something. 'Here.' She pushed a pound coin into the girl's palm.

'How about you lot?' the girl asked.

'You've got a pound,' McKay replied. 'Be merry with that, you liccle hustler.'

The girl grinned and skipped on.

'Step it up!' Boy from the Hills hollered from thirty metres up the path. 'Five-forty-nine.'

We rolled past the basketball court with our faces pointing in the opposite direction.

Festus's face grew large in my head.

I couldn't help but steal a glimpse through the meshed fence.

The players were taking a timeout. None of them looked like Festus.

Thank God!

One of them sat on the ball. They sank bottles of water that the girls had brought.

My nerves screamed at me to run, but I managed to

compose myself. Bit stepped quicker and led us around the perimeter fence.

The red-bricked library was in clear view. It was a tall building with lots of points and angles that my maths teacher would've loved. Thirteen steps led to the glass door entrance. A board fixed on its outer wall displayed its opening and closing times.

'Jonah, you step in with the girls,' Boy from the Hills suggested. 'McKay and Bit, keep a lookout here. But don't make it look as if you're looking out.'

'How do we do that?' McKay wanted to know.

'I dunno,' replied Boy from the Hills. 'I thought you had top ratings for drama.'

'Just pretend you're waiting for a friend to go into the library,' said Saira.

'Why would I wait outside for a friend?' McKay asked. 'I'd wait inside.'

'This is getting us nowhere,' I said. 'Just chill!'

I led the way up the steps. Saira and Venetia followed.

I pushed through the doors. I couldn't explain it but I had this vibe that something was wrong.

Everything was quiet, apart from the sound of the air conditioning and whispered conversations. Peeps were parked at desks reading newspapers and magazines. Kids did their homework. Staff sat behind counters stamping books and sipping beverages. In a corner, an ancient couple played chess. A toddler played with alphabet blocks in the children's zone. She was having a proper good time.

The beige walls looked as if they had been given a recent coat of paint.

There was no sniff of Juniper or the two girls who had been watching the football game.

Oh no. Maybe those North Crongton sisters have kidnapped her?

'Where the fruck is she?' Venetia wanted to know.

'Maybe she went to the toilet?' Saira wondered.

'She might've left already and is looking for us,' I said.

'Has this place got another exit?' I asked.

I decided to approach the counter.

'Is this the only part of the library?' I asked the man behind the desk. 'And . . . and do you have a toilet?'

'Yes, we do,' replied the librarian. He pointed near to the children's zone. 'There's a short hallway where the toilets are, and the hallway leads to the reference library.'

'Thank you,' Saira said.

'Are you members here?' the man asked.

'Er . . . no,' I replied.

We followed the librarian's directions. 'Would you like to become members?'

We ignored the question.

We checked the toilets. Someone had left an unflushed number two. No one was inside.

At the end of the hallway, we pushed through double swing doors.

It opened out into a bigger room. Desks and chairs covered the floor space. Tall bookshelves filled the sides.

Late sunlight streamed through the high windows. Peeps my age and above studied textbooks and typed on laptops and tablets. They scribbled down notes and looked proper serious. It was hard to imagine I was still in North Crongton.

'Is it the same game in South Crong Library?' I asked.

'Yep,' replied Saira. 'Full of study folk. Sometimes I step there just to get a liccle peace doing my homework.'

'Now, where is she?' asked Venetia.

Saira spotted Juniper first. She had parked at a desk and was reading something. We waved at her, but she didn't see us. I hot-stepped towards her.

'No running!' A woman behind a counter raised her voice at me.

I reached Juniper. She was enjoying a graphic novel. 'What are you doing?' I asked.

'Reading,' Juniper replied. 'That's what peeps do in libraries.'

'You're supposed to be getting the book!'

'I've got it,' Juniper confirmed.

'Where is it?' Saira wanted to know.

'Wrapped up in the plastic bag,' Juniper revealed. 'There's some secret-service spy shit going down. You're not gonna believe what's inside.'

'What do you mean?' asked Venetia. 'What's inside?'

Juniper grinned. 'You'll see.'

'You've got the book,' I said. 'So, let's bounce outta here. The others are waiting outside.'

'Shall I take this graphic novel with me?' Juniper asked. 'The story's got a flow and the pics are on point. I wanna finish it. Maybe I should ask to be a member of this place?'

'No!' I raised my voice. 'We haven't got time for that. Let's go missing.'

Juniper stood up, cut her eyes at me and left the graphic novel on the desk. She led the way through the double doors and into the main library. We passed the staff counter. The man who had given us directions followed us with his eyes. He didn't look friendly.

'Are you a member of this library?' he asked Juniper. 'Are you going to check that book out before you leave?'

Before I could think of a reply, Juniper took off as if our chemistry teacher wanted homework from her. Saira and Venetia hot-toed after Juniper. For a short second I froze to the spot. The library assistant shook his head at me before moving towards the counter gate. I didn't wait to see if he wanted to check if I had jacked a book.

I blazed through the glass doors, bounced down the steps, swiped Juniper's bag from her grasp and didn't stop until I was a safe distance past the basketball court.

It took a short while for the others to catch up with me. Venetia reached me first. 'What's wrong with you?' she panted. 'Why did you burn off like that?'

'I didn't start running,' I said. 'Juniper did.'

Liccle Bit arrived next. 'Have you got it?' he asked. 'Have you got it?'

'Yes.' I grinned. 'I've got it.'

'Let's have a look,' Saira asked.

I pulled the book out of the bag. I spotted a folded-up piece of paper sticking out from the pages.

'*Don't* take it out here!' Boy from the Hills warned. He and Saira had just caught up with us. 'We'll look at it when we get to McKay's.'

'Where's McKay?' I asked.

We looked towards the basketball court. McKay stepped around the perimeter fence as if he were out for a Sunday morning stroll with the Crongton Heath walking club.

'Put your toes in gear!' shouted Boy from the Hills. 'We're waiting on you.'

Eventually, McKay joined us. 'I'm not sure if I should spend my good time with you crims,' he laughed.

'Why didn't you run?' I asked.

'I never t'iefed the book,' he replied. 'Why should I sweat up myself? Can I have a look at it?'

I also wanted to check out this *16Lives* thing, but as soon as I took it out from the bag, Boy from the Hills went into dictator mode. 'Not here!' he yelled again. 'Put it back!'

'All right, all right,' I said. 'Don't bust a blood vessel.'

We rolled by Sugar Minott's. Kerb-rats were still parked on the low wall. They munched their crisps and chocolate bars. Next to them, a guy about sixteen, maybe seventeen, sat on his bike sinking a pattie. Pastry crumbs surrounded his lips. He scoped us as we passed. 'Man, we're living in desperate times,' he said. 'Ghetto peeps start jacking shit from libraries.'

I guessed he had seen us hot-foot from the library.

'It must be some book,' bike guy said. 'I feel that. I can't be bothered to fill out forms and stuff to get shit outta the library.'

Damn. This is gonna go all wrong.

My heart booted my ribcage. My senses told me to pin my head back, pray for sweet Jesus and scorch all the way home to South Crong.

'Keep cool,' whispered Boy from the Hills. 'We're just bouncing about our everyday business.'

The crew on the wall gazed at us before one of them laughed and said, 'Only in North Crong.'

'I don't wanna hang in these ends in Dracula time,' I whispered.

'I'm with you on that one.' Bit nodded.

We headed towards the North Crongton ring road and didn't look back. The sun dipped beneath the tall slabs and the streetlights flickered on.

We made it to the roundabout. The smell of the kebab shop licked my nostrils.

'I'm not gonna wait on no bus,' I said. 'We're still too close to enemy ends.'

Saira and Venetia swapped a glance before they nodded.

'Jonah's right,' Venetia said. 'And I can still sniff that shit on the green even here at the bus stop. Let's bounce.'

Twenty minutes later, we stepped into the lift in McKay's slab. Not sure what it was but it stank of something.

'Can I have a look at it now?' Saira asked.

'No!' said Boy from the Hills. 'You never know who might step in the lift.'

As soon as the lift doors opened, we hot-stepped to McKay's gates. But McKay took his own good time. He opened the door and slapped on a light. McKay's game consoles covered the sofa. Folded-up clothes sat on an armchair. We made our way to the kitchen table. Juniper and Saira shared a seat. Boy from the Hills, Bit and Venetia filled the other chairs. McKay took something out of the fridge. A souvenir magnet of Warwick Castle stuck to a corner of the fridge door. McKay's herbs, seasonings and spices were in cute little jars on a shelf. A mug with a Scottish flag printed on it rested on the draining board.

I decided to stand.

I unfolded the plastic bag and placed the book on the table. I stepped back a pace. There was a hush. We stared at it for a long second. The cover image was a profile of a neat-looking white brother. He wore a suit, a white shirt and a tie.

'Looks boring,' said Juniper. 'I wouldn't read it. I should've swiped that graphic novel too.'

I opened the book.

Spikes on a kite.

I wasn't even aware that my mouth opened wide. The knot in my stomach grew tentacles. They tightened around my guts. I blinked and shook my head. My eyes didn't betray me. What I saw was real.

The pages of the book had been hollowed out with a sharp blade. In their place was a thick wad of twenty-pound notes bound by an elastic band.

'Oh my good gosh,' said Venetia. 'That's a whole heap of money.'

'Allah is good.' Saira smiled. 'Very good.'

'So is Buddha, Hare Krishna, Yoda and the Stonehenge folk,' added Boy from the Hills.

'And Jesus,' put in Venetia.

'How much is there?' Bit asked. 'How much?'

'Enough to buy a hundred pairs of pink Dr. Martens,' said Juniper. 'I told you this is some kinda CIA, MI5, James-Bond kinda shit. Look at the pages! Cleanly cut. No raggedy edges. Wouldn't surprise me if there was a drone scoping us through a window.'

I couldn't help but peer through the kitchen window.

'So, all those peeps who study in the library didn't have a clue about a book that was stuffed with money,' said Saira. 'Imagine that? A jackpot was only an arm's length away.'

'Don't think too many North Crong Library folk are studying Irish history,' replied Boy from the Hills.

'Lucky for us,' said Venetia.

'Lucky?' I repeated. 'It might be a curse.'

Boy from the Hills picked up the notes. He held them to the light and examined them. 'There are grands here! Four. Maybe five.'

McKay came over and snatched the wad from Boy from

the Hills' hands. 'It might be fake,' he said. 'Isn't there supposed to be some kinda silver strip?'

McKay studied a note close up. 'It's got a silver foil and that watermark thing.'

He turned it over. 'Some brother called J. M. W. Turner,' McKay said. 'Never heard of him.'

'It looks real to me,' Venetia said. 'Juniper, would your pops accept it in your shop?'

'He most certainly would.' Juniper nodded. 'It's as real as the fox shit near our bins.'

McKay peeled off the elastic and grabbed the cash with both hands. 'I've always wanted to do this.' He smiled.

Suddenly, McKay threw the money up in the air and closed his eyes. It rained twenty-pound notes. Saira leaped from her chair and picked up ten of them. She tickled Venetia's nose with it. 'We're rich!'

Bit, Juniper and Boy from the Hills joined the fun until everyone was smacking each other with hard cash. Saira chased me around McKay's breakfast table until I tripped over. She licked my neck with a wad of twenties. Bit did a dance with his hands gripping wads of cash.

Christ on a hike! If I give a slice of my share to Pops, he'll never have to worry about stepping back into our yard again. Mum will be hugging him before she can open the next bill.

'Hold on!' Boy from the Hills cried. 'Hold on!'

'Hold on for what?' Bit asked.

'The note.' Boy from the Hills pointed to the book. 'What's on the note?'

Saira pulled out the folded paper from inside the book and everyone took their seats again. The hush returned. She opened it. The gremlin banged my tonsils once more. She read a few lines to herself before she looked up and searched our eyes. 'Interesting,' she said. 'Very interesting. Manjaro's one messed-up brother.'

'What does it say?' McKay urged. 'What does it say?'

'That whoever finds the money will be deleted, snipped into small pieces and fed to the froth-mouthy hounds on Crongton Heath,' I guessed.

'Thank you, Mr Negative,' Venetia snapped.

'I'm not being negative,' I argued. 'Just being real. Who knows who else is hunting for this money?'

Saira cleared her throat.

'It might be Major Worries,' I suggested. 'Or Festus?'

'*Shut up!*'

Saira side-eyed me and sucked in a breath.

'"So, you get brave and step into North Crong. I have to give ratings for that. I know what happened with Festus and his crew. Even Major Worries said that was a wrong move – we made a deal to keep juvenile civilians out of our beef. Festus pissed on that rule. He took it too far. He deserved to get gored. He's a rogue soldier. Major Worries sent out an order that McKay and his bredrens couldn't be touched. We agreed on that shit."'

I breathed out my relief.

'There's more,' said Saira.

'Read it then,' urged McKay. 'Don't stop.'

The North Crongton Library Mission

'"I'm a bit of a socialist at heart, so I hope you've all learned something on this mission. It took me untold hours putting this shit together. But no worries – a man's gotta do something to fill his time when he's on a low profile. You now have a choice to make. To keep what you have and share it out. Or, take it to the final act. Who wants to go on? There's a treasure chest out there. Yo-ho-ho and a bottle of Jamaican rum and all that. And that's no lie. Sometimes the adventurous get rewarded. Ask Jim Hawkins."'

'Who in the world of Crongton is Jim Hawkins?' asked Bit.

'Maybe one of his crew?' I guessed. 'Maybe this Jim bruv did something for Manjaro?'

'He sounds like one of them bird-watching folk,' said Juniper.

'Manjaro's playing us,' said McKay.

'Maybe,' said Venetia. 'Maybe not. He didn't play with the cash he left us to find.'

'How much money we got now?' I asked. 'Let's call it game over and count it. We have more than enough to put something towards the youth club building.'

'They're gonna interrogate us about where we got that kinda money from,' said Bit. 'They're not gonna believe that we found half of it in Crongton Park and the other half in a fricking library book.'

'I'm gonna put my share towards a fund,' said Venetia. 'For families who have lost . . . you know.'

My parents will ask untold questions about where I got the funds from. Maybe I can take the bills, quickstep to the post office and pay them myself.

'I'm gonna help delete our debts,' I said.

'I hear that,' said Boy from the Hills. 'I'm gonna slap mine on top of Venetia's fund.'

'Where's the rest of it?' Juniper wanted to know. 'Those notes you found in the woods in Crongton Park?'

'In a safe at the bottom of my wardrobe,' replied Boy from the Hills. 'Only I know the combination.'

'You've got a fricking safe?' I wanted confirmation.

Boy from the Hills nodded. 'Yep.'

'What's inside it?' I pressed.

Boy from the Hills stared at the floor.

'Don't you wanna hear what the rest of the note says?' asked Saira. 'There's some sort of rhyme.'

'Rhyme?' I repeated. 'Manjaro's some kind of grime artist?'

'Go on!' urged McKay.

Saira studied the words. Silence fell again.

'They called me bad, they called me sad, but I was never
  a liar
Read my words keenly if you wanna reach your desire.
Dive off the bridge if you wanna take it down to the
  wire
You're gonna have to get wet in the middle of the fire.
Down to the bed

There you will find purple bread.
You have to step north from the north
Beware of the ugly one and the wolf.'

'What in the name of Jamie Oliver is all that about?' wondered McKay.

'I haven't a damn diddly,' I said.

'It's a riddle,' said Boy from the Hills. 'We have to try to work it out.'

'It's gobbledegookery,' said Venetia.

'Don't make no sense to me,' added Saira. 'North from north? You have to get wet in the middle of the fire?'

'You guys can work on that riddle,' said McKay. 'I'm gonna hustle up some salmon. I can't think on an empty stomach.'

McKay took out a bowl from a cupboard and seasoned the fish with mixed herbs and garlic.

Boy from the Hills and Saira re-read Manjaro's riddle but couldn't make any rhyme or reason out of it.

'"Dive off the bridge if you wanna take it down to the wire,"' Saira repeated. '"There you will find purple bread"?'

'"North from north"?' asked Boy from the Hills. 'What does that mean?'

'He's laughing at us,' I said. 'Can't we be merry with what we've got? We all have enough to do what we wanna do.'

'I am merry,' replied Boy from the Hills. 'But it's chewing me.'

'It's gonna munch you to the end of your days,' said Venetia. 'Maybe we should let it go.'

'Yes!' I agreed. 'Let's not get too grabilicious.'

Boy from the Hills shook his head.

McKay, who had pulled on his mum's fave apron, whistled in the background as he carefully prepared our meal.

'Let's count it,' suggested Boy from the Hills.

Saira helped Boy from the Hills tally the cash. They licked their fingers.

'Eight grand exactly,' Saira said five minutes later. She couldn't kill her grin. 'Eight fricking grand! Altogether that's ten Gs.'

'I'll buy purple *and* pink Dr. Martens.' Juniper smiled. 'And a saxophone. I've always wanted to learn to play a saxophone. I'll busk at Crongton Central. Who knows? One day I'll be blowing melodies at the Shenk-I-Sheck club.'

'I'll tell you what,' said Boy from the Hills. 'We'll sleep on it. If anyone can work out the riddle, they've got until twelve-thirty tomorrow – lunchtime. We'll share after that. Everyone on that?'

'I'm on that.' I nodded.

Gosh. How much is ten Gs shared by six peeps? It's at least a grand and a half if my maths isn't all wrong. It'll certainly bless up the fam finances.

'Me too,' said Bit.

'And me,' added Venetia.

'It's still messing with me.' Saira shook her head. 'There's a treasure chest out there waiting for us.'

'I can picture it,' replied Boy from the Hills. 'How would you feel if someone else found it?'

'Not good,' Venetia admitted. 'We've done all the hard work.'

'Everyone take a pic of the riddle,' suggested Boy from the Hills. 'Remember, lunchtime tomorrow.'

'More homework,' grumbled Juniper. 'I'm soooo behind on my school stuff.'

I took out my phone and snapped the riddle. It hurt my head to even think about it.

Forty-five minutes later, McKay served us our meal of roast salmon, asparagus and mashed potato. I couldn't lie – it was proper delicious with a big D.

'Any dessert?' wondered Juniper.

'Dessert?' McKay repeated. 'Dessert? Liberties!'

'I was wondering about that too,' said Venetia. 'A meal like that deserves a serious dessert to follow it.'

We all nodded.

'I'm forever hustling up something for you guys,' said McKay. 'The next time we bounce into Barrington's Diner or the Cheesecake Lounge, I ain't buying shit. *You* can buy it for me.'

'I haven't got no argument with that,' said Venetia.

'Me neither,' agreed Saira.

'Gonna have to start saving for the portions *you* want,' I joked.

Boy from the Hills washed up the dishes and I dried up.

'I have to step now,' said Boy from the Hills. He picked

up the money and banked it in his backpack. 'Mum's got someone important she wants me to meet this evening.'

'Who's that when he's sinking champagne in a corner?' asked Bit.

'Some local politician,' replied Boy from the Hills. 'He wants to know how young peeps feel about amenities on the Heath.'

'Boring!' said Juniper.

'Anyway,' said Boy from the Hills. 'Twelve-thirty tomorrow. Get your thinking hoods on.'

'Don't get jacked on the way home,' I said. 'That'll be most tragic.'

'I won't,' he said as he left.

The rest of us stared at each other, not quite believing that nearly an hour ago, we smacked each other with twenty-pound notes.

'I'm gonna think on this,' promised Saira. 'It's probably simple.'

'It might as well have been written in Mongolian,' I said.

'Or Klingon,' added Juniper. 'Gonna catch up with *Doctor Who* on iPlayer when I reach my gates.'

Everyone laughed.

17

Things Fall Apart

I made it home just before eight-thirty.

Heather and Mum sat in the kitchen. They sipped coffee. They didn't speak much. Instead, they gazed at each other as if they were waiting for some end of world doom. Maybe *my-house-is-better-than-yours* Aunt Sonya had announced a visit.

'Jonah.' Mum smiled at me. 'Sorry, I didn't cook today. If you like I can fry up some sausages and eggs. I think there's a tin of baked beans in the cupboard.'

'That's all right, Mum,' I replied. 'I had something at McKay's.'

'Are you sure?' Mum asked. 'It's no bother.'

'I'm sure, Mum. I'm good. Had salmon, mash and aspara-something.'

'Asparagus,' corrected Heather. 'Maybe McKay can

teach you to cook?'

I heard a noise from Mum's room.

'Dad home?' I asked.

Heather nodded. She reached out for Mum's hands. She squeezed them gently. Mum closed her eyes for a long moment as if reliving a painful memory.

I stepped into Mum's room. The varnished wooden cross she had on the wall overlooking her bed was still there. The open Bible had kept its place on the dressing table – Mum underlined important passages with a pink marker. Her old-school radio sat beside it. I sniffed the faint scent of an incense stick.

An open suitcase was on the bed. Dad's clothes were packed inside. His toiletry bag sat next to it. His blue toothbrush was well-worn. He was about to place his copy of Chinua Achebe's *Things Fall Apart* in the zipped-up compartment of his suitcase. He had forever recommended the book to me, but I hadn't got around to reading it.

I felt this surge of anger stream through me. We swapped an awkward glance.

'Jonah,' he said. 'I . . . I wanted to have finished my packing before you got home.'

'Why?' I asked. 'So you can sneak out the rest of your things when I'm not here?'

Dad met my fierce glare. 'I . . . I wanted to do this without so much fuss . . . and pain.'

I watched him pack his Fela Kuti CDs.

Things Fall Apart

'What... what if I found a bag of money?' I said. 'Say you could pay all your debts? Say you had no bills to pay? No money worries. Would you stay then?'

Dad thought about it. He slowly shook his head.

'How much money do we actually owe, Dad?' I added. 'Maybe I could... yeah, maybe I could borrow it from friends. We're tight like that. Just tell me how much it is.'

'It's not your responsibility.' Dad raised his voice. 'It's mine.'

'But if we get booted out of the flat cos we can't pay the rent, they're not gonna say I can stay cos it wasn't my responsibility. Let me ask my friends and see—'

'Jonah!' Dad yelled. 'That is enough! If you want to help, keep up with your schoolwork and your running. Don't waste your talent.'

I dropped my head. For a short moment I felt guilty about not giving the full one hundred per cent to my athletics. *When the end credits roll on my family situation, I'm gonna have to be a soldier for Mr Smallwood.*

'I'll be staying on longer at Uncle Levi's,' Dad said. 'And I hope to be in my own place soon. Wherever I am, you're always welcome to visit.'

'Who says I want to visit?'

'When... when things calm down,' Dad said. 'I'm sure you... you will come and see me. Once the shock... once emotions are not so raw.'

'You will continue to see your father,' shouted Mum from the kitchen. 'There's no blame here.'

Dad and I shared a long look. A tear formed in his left eye.

I couldn't take it any more. I marched out and headed for my own room. I slammed the door behind me and sat at the foot of my bed. I looked up at Usain Bolt. 'I don't know why,' I said. 'But I thought he might come back and stay.'

I crashed out for an hour until someone tickled my door. I didn't want to answer it but whoever it was slapped again.

'Who is it?' I asked. *No one ever knocks on my gates*.

'Heather. Can I come in?'

'I suppose so.'

Heather stepped in. She parked herself near my pillow. She folded her arms. She looked around my room before she caught my gaze.

'I thought he was gonna come back and stay,' I said.

Heather nodded. 'Me too,' she replied. 'It's nobody's fault. Maybe things have run their course for them. But Pops is still your pops . . . and mine.'

'Is he still here?' I asked.

Heather shook her head. 'He left about ten minutes ago. He said he'll talk to you another time. When things have . . . you know . . .'

'When emotions are not so raw,' I said.

'That's what he said.' Heather nodded.

'Do you really believe why they broke up was just about the stress of money?' I asked. 'Nobody else is involved . . . are they?'

Heather replied quick-time. 'No, no, no! There's no one else in Mum and Dad's drama.'

'If we found a stash of money and paid all the bills,' I wondered, 'would that help?'

'And where are we gonna find a cabin case of notes?' Heather wanted to know. 'I can barely find the funds to meet up with my friends and go out on a Friday evening.'

'Is that what you wanna do, sis? Go out on a Friday night?'

Heather nodded. 'Yeah, why not,' she replied. 'I study hard. I can't remember the last time I bought some new garms at Crongton Broadway and rolled out to enjoy myself.'

'It'll happen soon,' I promised. 'Trust me on that. I'll put something towards it.'

Heather laughed. 'Jonah, stop chatting foolishness!'

'I'm not.'

I thought about Manjaro's riddle. *I'm gonna study that mother till my eyes go strange.*

'Now, don't go on all dark with Pops,' Heather said. 'All because he doesn't wake up here – it doesn't mean he's gonna be a bad dad for you. He's not gonna go all ghost on us like other dads here in South Crong.'

'Can't they go to marriage guidance or something?' I suggested. 'Everything's happened so quick.'

Heather shook her head. 'Who knows how long they've been having their issues. Might be months. Years.'

She squeezed my shoulder and stood up. 'Nuff fams go

through this, Jonah,' she said. 'I remember the drama when Bit's dad left. Elaine's heart was mashed. I'm sure Bit was traumatised too. Now, it's our turn. We'll come out of it OK.'

My head dropped. Heather kissed me on the top of my forehead. 'Don't do anything cadazy and keep up your ratings with your schoolwork and running.'

'I'll try,' I replied.

'We're all gonna holler you on at the school regional champs.'

'You're all coming for that?'

'Yeah, of course.'

I closed the door behind Heather and still felt empty inside. I decided to call Saira.

'Hi, Jonah,' she greeted. 'You good?'

'Not completely,' I replied.

'Why? What's up?'

'Pops,' I said. 'He's just come back for his garms and other stuff. This ain't no timeout thing. He's left Mum for real.'

'Sorry to hear, Jonah. Real sorry. Do you want me to come around? Keep you company?'

Oh my days. She's never offered to come around to my gates before. What do I do? What do I say? Shit on a spit. I've gotta clean up my room.

'If it's not too late,' I said. 'That'll be great.'

'I wanna get out anyway,' Saira said. 'Mum's got a few of her friends around. She wants me to play the perfect daughter-hostess. If I stay any longer, I'll be asked to bake a cake or something and do the washing-up. I wanna work on Manjaro's riddle. It's still burning my brain.'

'That's gonna give me and you a headache,' I said. 'I'm on it. We've got ten Gs to share but that's only a little dose over a grand and a half each.'

'It might be more. A pirate's chest of money more.'

'It might be dangerous,' I reminded her. 'North Crongton wasn't a joke. That could've gone wrong.'

'I also wanna ask you something,' she said. 'A big favour.'

'A favour?' I repeated. 'Like what?'

'You'll find out when I reach.'

'OK,' I said. 'See you in . . .'

'Ten,' Saira completed the sentence.

18

The Big Ask

When I killed my call with Saira, I looked for Heather. She sat at the kitchen table sipping another hot drink. She stared into space. I guessed she was more shocked by Pops leaving with the rest of his stuff than I was.

Mum had gone to her room. I filled her chair. Heather lifted her head and switched her gaze on me. 'What is it?' she asked.

'Don't embarrass me,' I said. 'Please, please don't embarrass me.'

'Jonah, what on God's sweet earth are you whining on about?'

'I don't whine,' I argued.

'Yes, you do. You're a professional whiner. Times ten.'

'Saira,' I said. 'Saira's coming around.'

'That pretty Turkish girl?'

'Yep. Her.'

'Seriously? No jokes?'

'Yes, most seriously. Why do you think that's a joke?'

Heather checked the time on her phone. 'It's nearly ten o'clock.'

'She's not gonna stay long.'

'Trust me –' Heather raised her tones – 'if I have anything to do with it, she won't stay long. Not in your room anyway.'

'So *please* don't embarrass me.'

'Jonah, even if I wanted to shame you, I just haven't got the energy. When she arrives, be a gent and ask her if she wants a drink or anything to eat.'

I cleared the kitchen table, wiped it with a wet wipe and swept the floor. Heather shook her head as she watched me. 'Maybe you should invite a girl around every day. At least it gets you cleaning the place.'

'Are you going to your room?' I asked. 'I mean it – *don't* embarrass me.'

Heather chuckled before finally heading to her bedroom. *'Don't* take her inside your bedroom. I don't wanna be an aunt by next Sunday. Have you done sex education yet?'

'You're not funny.'

Nine minutes later, Saira slapped my gates.

Oh, shit. I didn't have enough time to scrub my molars. Hope my breath is not too toxic. Do I need to blast my armpits with deodorant?

I couldn't leave her waiting. I opened the door. Saira smiled at me. For a long second, I stood still, just admiring her, not quite believing that she was at my gates.

'Come in, come in,' I said.

I led her to the kitchen. She sat in Heather's chair. She unbuttoned her jacket.

'Do . . . do you want a hot drink . . . or something?'

'No, I'm good for now.'

'Are you sure? We've got coffee.'

'I'm sure, Jonah.'

I parked opposite her. I dared to gaze into her brown eyes. She had shaped her eyebrows into a delicious curve. Some kind of gloss blessed her lips. There was a dose of rouge redding up her cheeks. I wondered what it would be like to kiss her.

'How . . . how are you doing?' she asked.

'OK . . . I think. It was just a mega-shock to see him pack a suitcase.'

'Yeah.' She nodded. 'Of course, it's gonna be a shock to your core. It won't feel normal for a while, but it'll get better. Trust me on that one.'

'At least . . . at least I can still get to see him.'

Saira checked her nails. She was about to say something but stopped herself.

'Do . . . do you wanna cold drink?'

'Yeah,' she replied. 'What have you got?'

I should have checked before. I really hoped we had something. I stood up and went to the fridge and found a carton of apple juice. I shook it. There were enough dribbles to fill half a glass.

'Apple juice OK?'

Saira nodded.

I poured the juice into a glass. My heart pumped as if it wanted to escape my chest. I offered Saira her drink.

'Thanks.'

I sensed a touch of nerves in her eyes. 'At least . . . at least when Mum's got her friends around she doesn't have to stress out about Pops,' she said.

I didn't know how to respond to that.

'Yeah, I s'pose so,' I managed.

'You sure you're gonna be OK?' she asked. 'Remember, it's got nothing to do with you why your parents have split up. Don't forget that.'

'I won't.'

Saira sank half of her juice. She flicked her eyes at me before carefully placing the glass on the table.

'You . . . you said you want a favour?' I said. 'What's the favour?'

Saira read a message on her phone. She thought about something before switching it off. 'You might think I'm taking liberties,' she said.

'Liberties?' I repeated. 'About what?'

'We're good friends, right?' she asked.

'Yeah, course,' I replied. 'Obviously, I don't wanna be marooned in the friend zone for ever.'

'That's why this is so difficult.'

'What's difficult?' I pressed but my heart dropped like a stone statue in a calm sea. I didn't want to hear what she had to say next.

She took another sip from her glass. She sucked in a long breath. She placed the glass on the table. She studied the purple nail varnish on the index finger of her left hand.

'What's so difficult?' I asked again.

'Merlene,' she replied. 'Merlene Quarrie.'

'The runner?' I asked. 'What about her?'

She flicked her gaze to the fridge. 'How . . . how well do you know her?'

'Not too good,' I replied. 'Just from training. We haven't really chatted that much.'

'Has . . . has she got . . . someone?'

I noticed the urgency in her gaze. I sensed she wanted me to answer no. It was finally obvious to me what was going down.

'You like her?'

Saira dropped her gaze. 'Yeah.' She nodded. 'Big time. I'm well past the butterflies-in-my-stomach stage. I get *Jurassic Park* birds flying between my ribs when I see her. She's beautiful, don't you think?'

She smiled nervously.

'Er . . . yeah, course she is,' I replied. 'Where . . . where do I come in?'

Saira shrugged. 'I . . . I don't know if she, er . . . feels the same way, or even . . . er . . .'

'You don't know if girls are her thing,' I finished the sentence for her.

Saira nodded.

'And you want me to find out?'

She didn't respond for a long second.

'Saira?'

'We've looked at each other,' she said. 'You know . . . she smiled . . . but I'm not sure.'

'Never seen her with a guy,' I said. 'But you don't know what goes on behind the stage curtain.'

'Do . . . do you think you can find out?' she queried. 'I know I'm asking a lot.'

I thought about it. I couldn't lie. Disappointment booted my heart.

'What am I supposed to say?' I asked. 'Finish training, then bounce up to her and say, "Oh, by the way, do girls tickle your fancy or do guys do it for you?"'

'You're being flippant,' Saira accused.

She wasn't wrong.

We sat in silence for the next minute or so.

'I'll . . . I'll think of something,' I said. 'I dunno what. I'm not promising anything.'

Saira smiled. She reached out and squeezed my shoulders.

'I hope Merlene doesn't drop a pond-load of cold water over you,' I said. 'She'd have to be dead inside not to fancy you.'

'So, what are you saying?' she laughed. 'None of

Juniper's ghosts find me pretty?'

'Juniper and her ghosts?' I chuckled.

Suddenly, Saira peered into her glass as if she had found ten Gs inside it.

'What is it?' I asked.

'Pond-load,' she said. 'Oh my life! There's a pond in Fireclaw Heath!'

'Yeah.' I shook my head. 'So what?'

'And a small bridge!'

'What's this gotta do with Merlene Quarrie?' I wondered.

'Don't you get it?' she asked.

'Get what?'

'Manjaro's riddle.' Saira raised her tones.

I placed a hand over Saira's mouth. 'Sssshhh,' I whispered. 'Don't mention that name here.'

Saira leaned in closer to me. She met my eyes and lowered her tones. '"Dive off the bridge if you wanna take it down to the wire. You're gonna have to get wet in the middle of the fire." He must be referring to the small pond on Fireclaw Heath.'

I pulled out my phone and opened a map app. I zoomed in to Fireclaw Heath. On the north-west corner of the land was a coloured blue area. It was surrounded by Ravenswood.

'That's the pond.' Saira pointed. 'There's a bridge there.'

'It's miles away from the Ashburton Road,' I said. 'It's like proper wilderness. Only wolves, coyotes and strange walking folk go near it. How are we gonna get there? And how long is this bridge?'

Saira shrugged. 'Walk? I dunno. We'll find out how long it is when we get there.'

'It might be as long as that one in San Francisco,' I said.

Saira angled her head and pressed her lips together. 'Really, Jonah?'

'I can hear McKay blistering my ears with his moaning,' I said. 'He's not gonna slow-toe it all the way to the corners of Fireclaw Heath.'

'Bikes!' said Saira. 'Boy from the Hills has got his own but the rest of us can borrow a Crongton bike from the bus station.'

'You sure about this, Saira? It's well out of the ends. I've never planted a foot on Fireclaw Heath. I've heard some proper disturbing tings about that place. Buried bodies, Bigfoots and weird-looking rabbits.'

'What's a Bigfoot?'

'Some long ugly hairy ting with bungalow-size feet.'

'At least we don't have to worry about crashing into North Crong kerb-rats,' Saira said. 'You're not afraid of the dark, are you?'

'Course not.'

'Then what's the problem?'

I thought about it. 'Do you know how deep that pond is?'

'Can't be that deep,' she replied. 'We're not gonna find the Loch Ness monster down there. Or a giant squid.'

'Might find Juniper's ghosts,' I joked.

Saira burst out laughing.

'Another mission,' I said.

Saira grinned. 'Yeah, dramatic, isn't it?'

'And dangerous.'

Saira stood up. 'Glad we solved the riddle.'

'We don't know yet.'

'I'm sure we have.'

I led her to the front door.

'Don't forget to, er . . . to drop two words in Merlene's ear corners.'

'I won't forget,' I promised. 'But if she's not feeling you, don't blame me.'

Another mission, I said to myself. *It's gonna be proper dangerous out there but the treasure chest might be heavier than all of Usain Bolt's gold medals.*

19

Fireclaw Heath

Saira had messaged everyone on the Crongton Knights WhatsApp group. Boy from the Hills said he'd work on a plan. I half expected him to bring a mini submarine. He advised us to bring a change of clothes – he didn't want anyone recognising us on the Heath from our school uniforms. McKay messaged that he'll be taking food supplies *in case we get lost*. Any wrong turning in Ravenswood and we'll be Hansel and Gretelled.

Who in the name of Bear Grylls is Hansel and Gretel? Saira wanted to know.

A couple of young peeps in a children's book who went on a mission into the forest and got kidnapped by a witch, replied Venetia.

Did they escape? Saira asked.

Can't remember, Venetia replied. I think a farmer or

somebody chopped off the witch's head.

Juniper warned us about the demons and duppies in the wild places of Fireclaw Heath. She also offered to bring an axe, a tent, fireworks and a smoke bomb. She didn't explain why she needed the smoke bomb. We declined.

Venetia wondered what to wear, and Liccle Bit admitted that if his sister, Elaine, discovered that his short ass was on Fireclaw Heath, he'd rather share a boxing ring with Major Worries than face her. **Let's keep this mission between us**, he said. **Don't even spill to yourself.**

Venetia sent a short reply.

Lol

Maybe them two are back on point?

We agreed to finalise plans in a corner of the dining room at school.

It was lasagne day but the dish wasn't up to McKay's ratings. 'If this mince was any more undercooked, it would've bounced off my plate, hot-trotted to the field and nibbled the grass!'

The food wasn't delicious, but it filled a hole.

We had to raise our voices above the clattering of knives, forks, plates and teachers stopping feuds kicking off.

'Vincent Chapman!' Ms Holmes screamed. 'Do we have to give you a bib? The food is meant to go in your mouth! Clean that mess off the floor!'

Boy from the Hills parked opposite me with a notepad and pencil in hand. Juniper played some complicated war game on her phone, and McKay, pushing away his plate of lasagne, chomped half of his apple crumble.

'From the Ashburton Road, as the raven flies, it's three and a half miles to the pond,' Boy from the Hills revealed.

'Three and a half miles!' McKay repeated. 'That's *long*!'

'We'll be on bikes,' Liccle Bit said.

'It's still long,' McKay argued. 'I've got more weight to shift than you skinny folk.'

'We've agreed not to dip into the funds we've already got so how much is it to hire one of those Crongton bikes?' I asked. 'It might be outta my budget.'

'I'll use my card,' said Boy from the Hills. 'Pay me back later.'

'With what?' I pressed. 'All I've got in my pockets is dust.'

'Your parents let you have a card?' Venetia asked Boy from the Hills.

'Yep,' Boy from the Hills replied. 'They're not usually there when I get home from school. With the card I can order my dinner on my phone.'

'Would your parents notice if you bought a few garms in Crongton Broadway?' Saira smiled. 'We might kidnap you one day.'

'Yes, they would,' replied Boy from the Hills. 'They check the balance every week.'

'Booooo,' hollered Saira. 'Anyway, we'll be riding back from Fireclaw Heath with untold notes in our backpacks. We'll be able to pay off Boy from the Hills *and* give him a tip.'

Everyone laughed.

'When is this mission gonna fly?' asked Juniper. 'Hopefully not on a *Doctor Who* night.'

'Everyone good for tomorrow?' Boy from the Hills asked, ignoring her. 'Venetia? Any drama or dancing?'

'Nope,' Venetia confirmed. 'Got a big bag of homework but it can wait.'

'Jonah?' Boy from the Hills turned to me. 'Any running, training, chasing Smallwood to the top of Falcon Ridge?'

'Not tomorrow,' I replied. 'But if my fam finds out I've been on Fireclaw Heath, they'll blast my ears till my grandkids turn grey.'

'Then don't tell 'em,' said Saira. 'I'm not.'

'Hold on, hold on,' McKay said. 'I've got an issue with those Crongton bikes.'

'What's the issue?' Boy from the Hills wanted to know.

'The seats are uncomfortable,' McKay explained. 'Last time I rode on one of them, it nearly cut me a new crease. I walked strange for a week.'

'You walk strange anyway,' quipped Bit.

We fell about in hysterics.

'You lot are compassion free,' said McKay. 'It's a serious issue.'

'Can we get down to business?' asked Boy from the Hills.

'Yep, go ahead,' said Saira.

'Everyone bring a backpack with them,' advised Boy from the Hills. 'We don't know what we're picking up from the pond or how big it is.'

'This is all good,' I said. 'But you forgot something.'

'What?' asked Venetia.

'Who's gonna dive down into that toxic pond and pick up the goods?'

We all looked at each other.

'And it could be deep like one of them Scottish lochs,' I added. 'There's no bottom. If you keep on swimming down, you'll reach Australia.'

'It's well deep,' said Juniper. 'It could be like *Twenty Thousand Fathoms Beneath the Sea*! There might be all sorts of *Doctor Who* things at the bottom.'

Saira stood up. She searched our eyes. 'I . . . I can do it,' she said. 'But I need a wetsuit. I'm not gonna pollute my skin with whatever's in that damn pond.'

'I might be able to help with the wetsuit,' said Boy from the Hills. 'My mum's got one from when my parents went diving off a Greek island to explore some shipwreck.'

'What about goggles?' Saira asked.

'Got them too,' replied Boy from the Hills.

'So, we're all good to go,' said Venetia. 'I wonder how much money is down there? It might all be proper soggy.'

'That'll be tragic,' said McKay.

'One last thing,' said Boy from the Hills.

'What is it now?' pressed Juniper.

'We wanna get there before it gets dark,' said Boy from the Hills. He fixed his gaze on Juniper. 'So, nobody get a detention tomorrow.'

'Why's everyone looking at me?' protested Juniper.

At three-forty p.m. the next day, the Crongton Knights and I waited in the library as Juniper served a detention in the food technology department. We had changed out of our school uniforms.

'I knew it,' said Boy from the Hills. 'We should've told her to take today off.'

Apparently Juniper had said something about the amount of brown dye the food technology teacher, Ms Parfitt, slapped on her hair. 'It looks as if she painted it on with cheap brown paint,' Juniper had said. 'She should've gone for a second coat. She'd be better off wearing a wig or just shaving it all off.'

'Standard Juniper,' Liccle Bit said, shaking his head.

Saira and Venetia read a book each. Liccle Bit flicked through a graphic novel. McKay took out his lunchbox and sniffed his corned-beef sandwiches and a couple of fairy cakes he had baked last night.

I felt peckish.

'You don't want a book to read, Jonah?' Mr Baldwin, the librarian, asked.

'No, I'm good,' I replied.

'I hope we can get away from Fireclaw Heath before it gets dark,' Boy from the Hills said.

Thirty-five minutes later, Juniper strolled into the library. She had already changed into green dungarees, black Dr. Martens boots and a blue beret. 'Sorry, guys,' she said. 'Ms Parfitt's got ears like the Terminator. I only whispered about her hair. I mean, it's so obvious. She's got grey sideburns!'

Fireclaw Heath

'Can we go?' asked Boy from the Hills.

'Can I take out a book?' Juniper asked.

Boy from the Hills closed his eyes and shook his head.

Juniper loaned out some gory horror book, squeezed it into her backpack and led the way out.

We stopped off at Dagthorn's store to stock up on bottled water.

'So good you guys are helping each other with your field geography,' Juniper's dad said.

Guilt smacked me on the forehead.

Field geography!

We stepped outside. It looked as if it was about to rain.

'You got the wetsuit?' Saira asked Boy from the Hills.

'Yep.'

'And the goggles?'

'Yep.'

'Got a submarine in there too?' I asked.

Boy from the Hills gave me a brutal side-eye.

Twenty minutes later, we arrived at Crongton Central bus station. Shoppers, carrying bags of garms from the Broadway shopping centre, waited under the arched, see-through bus shelter. Others sank hot drinks at the nearby Mr Mancini's Coffee and Cake House.

On a side-road behind the bus station was a bike stand. The bikes had been in use for more than ten years, but they had to change the colour from blue to a neutral green as North Crongton folk complained. Gang codes pollute everything in Crongton.

In The Ends

Boy from the Hills did his thing with his bank card. We mounted our bikes. They definitely didn't have as many gears as Boy from the Hills' name-brand cycle, which looked like something they rode at the Olympics.

Something slithered between my ribs and nibbled my heart as I thought about the ride to Fireclaw Heath and what we might find there. Boy from the Hills secured a phone grip to his handlebars. He punched in the postcode of our destination. 'Ready or not?' he asked.

McKay fidgeted uncomfortably on his seat. 'Should've brought some kind of seat pad,' he grumbled. 'Even a towel would've worked. I'm gonna be walking weird again.'

'We're ready!' said Saira. 'Crongton Knights in motion to Fireclaw Heath!'

'Hold on,' I said. 'Have these bikes got a light?'

Boy from the Hills showed me where the front light was. He switched it on. I glanced up at the sky and a dark blanket of greyness stared back at me.

'Let's roll,' said Boy from the Hills.

We took the Ashburton Road that led to the Crongton Circular. We cycled close to the kerb as we navigated the Crongton Green roundabout. We passed the exit to North Crongton and headed north, rejoining the Ashburton Road.

Boy from the Hills set a strong pace. McKay struggled to keep up. 'Why are you lot zooming off as if you're in the Tour de France?'

The avenues and cul-de-sacs of South Ashburton

came into view on our right-hand side. Range Rovers and other four-wheel drives niced up the parking bays outside neat front gardens. Junior kids who attended school there wore blazers with red and yellow trims and hats and bonnets.

On our left, the roads and houses quit. In their place was wild scrubland before it evened out into playing fields. I glanced behind and I could still see the lights from the tall slabs of North Crongton twinkling beyond the circular road. Looking to my left, I could barely make out the touchlines and markings of three sloping football pitches. The goalposts and crossbars were bent. The shed-like changing rooms were covered in North Crong graffiti.

'Can we stop a sec?' asked McKay.

Boy from the Hills raised his right hand and braked.

We sank water and rested our bones. Boy from the Hills pointed to Fireclaw Heath. In the distance, all we could see was endless clusters of trees that gradually climbed to the horizon. The clouds seemed to hang low over the area. It might have been a mist that refused to quit.

'The Ghoul Ends!' Juniper cried out. 'Duppy central.'

'Everyone ready?' Boy from the Hills asked.

We set off again.

We rode for another mile or so before we made a left on to a narrow path in Fireclaw Heath. Tall lampposts, spaced about thirty metres apart, had their lights already on.

The grass was untamed here, climbing to waist height in places. What trees there were grew on their lonesome.

They had lost most of their leaves. Away from the traffic, I heard the calling of birds above. I spotted a dog walker returning to the main road. She was the only person I could see on the Heath. The breezes seemed stronger, occasionally gusting and unbalancing me. The grass moved like a rolling wave when the wind blew hard. Ahead, the path wriggled this way and that like a long grey ribbon.

Pedalling west, the land steadily rose. There were thick bushes and clumps of nettles. The route curved to the right. We reached the top of a rise and took a breather. Peering north, I made out the lights of the Notre Dame estate. I couldn't see the slabs, only dark outlines and shadows. *Well happy we're not going there!*

Westward, the land suddenly dipped. We picked up speed. When we reached the valley, we could no longer see the Ashburton Road.

My heart banged a quicker beat. *Someone could delete us here and nobody would see.*

We came to a cross path.

'Do you know where you are?' I asked.

Boy from the Hills stopped. He checked the app on his phone. One route led from north to south and the other east to west. I couldn't see a signpost. 'We're on the right path,' he said. 'Keep going west.'

'Are you sure?' I queried. 'Looks like wilderness central.'

I stared ahead and could make out the fringes of Ravenswood – a shadow of dark green and brown. It seemed to suck in the light. The trees were taller there. Intimidating.

They dared us to enter. Now I understood why Juniper believed there were ghosts and duppies on Fireclaw Heath.

We rode on, slightly downhill. The breezes stilled.

I noticed that the grass was sparse here. What there was grew in tufts here and there among the mud pools and squelchy puddles. Blackbirds used their beaks to hunt for anything they could find. Their carking was loud and unnerving.

The lampposts had quit and so did the concrete path. It was now a skinny mud trail that curled to the left and steadily ascended. We rode in single file. McKay panted in front of me. Our wheels turned brown. The trees were much closer together. Strong gusts had shoved wet leaves into deep hollows and against steep banks. I guessed some wayward pilot had dropped cluster bombs here long ago.

I sniffed the scent of tree bark. Wild bushes appeared, thick enough to hide a posse of gangsters on the run. I heard living things on the ground but couldn't see them. Birds winged above our heads. Our lights shone brighter in the late afternoon dusk.

'Is this . . . ?' Venetia asked. 'Is this the world as we know it? This place seems . . . ancient.'

'Yes, it is,' replied Boy from the Hills. 'We're on the edge of Ravenswood. The pond is about a mile into it.'

'A mile!' repeated McKay.

As soon as we entered the forest, the grey light quit. Boy from the Hills switched his phone beam on. On either side of the path, the grass was short and pale. It was drier, with only the odd shallow puddle. We descended for another half mile or so before climbing again. We spotted the lights of houses in the distance but before we reached them, the track arced to the right.

'We're heading north again,' said Boy from the Hills.

'Are we there yet?' asked McKay. 'My legs are killing me!'

'Almost.'

Five minutes later, I heard something. It sounded like a voice, but I wasn't too sure, so I didn't say anything.

'What was that?' Saira asked. 'Somebody's out there.'

Boy from the Hills braked. He climbed off his bike and turned to us. Concern marked his forehead. He pressed his right index finger to his lips. He crept forward.

The trail sloped downhill. Midges and other tiny things buzzed in the air. A squirrel hot-pawed up a tree.

Boy from the Hills stopped, stood still and concentrated. 'Take your bikes off the path,' he advised. 'I'm gonna check this out.'

'Check what out?' I asked. 'I'm coming with you.'

'And me too,' said Juniper.

'And me,' added Venetia.

'OK,' agreed Boy from the Hills. 'Let's all go but be *quiet*. Let's find a place to hide our bikes.'

'Can't we stop and have something to eat?' asked McKay.

McKay was ignored.

We left the path and rolled our bikes over soft wet ground. The tyres collected damp, crinkly leaves.

'Should've worn boots,' Venetia said.

'Wellington boots,' I added.

We found a prickly bush about one and a half metres high and two metres wide. 'Lay the bikes here,' Boy from the Hills suggested. 'Cover them with the leaves. Put your phones on silent.'

We did what we were told.

'Keep low,' Boy from the Hills said. 'We're gonna climb up that slope.'

Boy from the Hills pointed the way before leading us to a mud bank. It was steep and slippery, but we managed to maintain a hold. Weeds and wild leaves grew out of it. Soil and grit clogged my fingernails. A row of five pine trees stood tall beyond the rise. The tips of the branches kissed the darkening skies.

'The pond's the other side,' whispered Boy from the Hills.

As I climbed, the air changed. It was cooler.

I heard someone speak. I had listened to that voice before. Something cold Lewis Hamiltoned through my veins. The slabs of Notre Dame estate stood tall in my mind.

'I can't believe it,' said Venetia. 'I'll *never* forget *him*.'

'*Who?*' wondered Juniper.

'G-Gore,' replied Venetia. 'It was him that jacked our phones in the Notre Dame estate. He is one dog-hearted, bullying, evil waste of a living space! I promised myself that if I ever saw that dirty rodent again, I'd stamp on his nuts!'

'Keep your voice down,' Boy from the Hills warned.

We popped our heads over the mud bank. About seventy

metres away, set lower than ground level, was the pond. It was shaped in a figure of eight, about thirty metres long and five metres wide at its narrowest point. It was very still. A wooden bridge spanned the water in the middle with rails about waist height. It had four steps leading up to it on either side. I guessed they had built it for anglers. Notre Dame graffiti was sprayed all over it – the letter H.

Standing on the bridge was G-Gore. He wore a grey beanie hat, a black duffel coat with large barrel-shaped buttons and black boots. I counted fifteen of his Hunchbacker crew standing on the grass in front of him. Another was lying face down on the bridge. He was naked from the waist up.

'Oh my living days!' I gasped.

'What in the frying universe are they doing to that bruv?' McKay wondered.

'You don't see *this* in *Top Boy*,' Saira said.

'Are they gonna fling him into the water?' Juniper fretted. 'And drown him?'

'Maybe they've deleted him already?' Liccle Bit suggested. 'He ain't moving.'

'Sssshhhh.' Boy from the Hills pressed his finger to his lips again. 'It looks like some kinda ceremony.'

'This isn't good,' I said. 'You've got the whole of the Notre Dame crew near the bridge where we're supposed to be diving. Can't we come back another time? Aren't you guys interested in living another day?'

'After I pedalled all the way from Crong bus station?'

McKay protested. 'No friggin way! Not before I sink my corned-beef roll anyway.'

'Maybe they know about Manjaro's treasure?' I put forward. 'Maybe that brother is gonna dive in and hunt for it?'

'I don't think so,' said Boy from the Hills. 'He's not wearing a swimming costume and I don't see any goggles. We'll wait.'

'Yes, we'll wait.' Saira nodded.

'But it's gonna get dark soon,' I said. 'Can you imagine what G-Gore and his crew will do to us if they see us? They'll tie a mountain to our ankles and fling us in the pond too!'

I was ignored.

Boy from the Hills took out his binoculars. 'It's definitely G-Gore.' He pointed. 'I can see the zits on his face.'

'What's he doing?' Bit asked.

'I dunno,' Boy from the Hills replied. 'He's just stepping around the bruv on the ground.'

Suddenly, G-Gore shouted. 'The bell!'

A guy, who was even shorter than Liccle Bit, came forward with a brass-coloured bell. In his other hand he carried what looked like a hammer.

'I've now been in this country for a few years,' said Saira. 'And I still find some of your ways messed up ... proper messed up.'

'Trust me, Saira,' I said. 'This is not one of our ways. Don't normalise this shit.'

'Frigging off-key kerb-bandits!' Venetia raised her voice. 'They should all be locked up.'

'Ssssshhhh.'

G-Gore accepted the hammer thing. He then clanged the bell as if he wanted to wake up some dead uncle in a dungeon. 'The first commandment!'

In the next moment, the Hunchbackers spoke as one. *'No Hunchbacker will ever snitch on a fellow Hunchbacker. If any Hunchbacker commits this grievous sin, then slow torturous death awaits him.'*

'The second commandment!' G-Gore bellowed.

'No Hunchbacker shall ever covet the girlfriend of any other Hunchbacker.'

'The third commandment!'

'Any possessions and property that you own belong to all Hunchbackers.'

'This is proper sick,' said Venetia. 'Boys and their toys! Does G-Gore think he's Moses? Is he gonna try and part the freaking pond? Is this what the North Crong and South Crong do too?'

'Something like it,' replied Bit. 'Every gang has their own initiation ceremony, I suppose.'

'Sssssshhhhh!'

'Your shushing is louder than us chatting,' McKay pointed out.

'The fourth commandment!' G-Gore roared.

'All Hunchbackers must commit to forever hating the North Crong, South Crong and especially the Poverty Driven Orphans

of Ashburton. We vow to wipe them off our lands when they plant their infidel toes upon it.'

I didn't like the sound of that. It wasn't funny any more.

'Poverty Driven Orphans?' repeated Boy from the Hills. 'Who are they when they piss on the bike sheds?'

'A young Ashburton crew,' replied Juniper. 'They start their gang careers early in those ends. Oldest member is about thirteen.'

'How do you know?' I asked.

'One of them came into our shop,' replied Juniper. 'When he gave me the money for an ice lolly, I could tell the PDO on his knuckles was written in biro. He looked about twelve.'

'The fifth commandment!'

'To reveal this initiation and the missions of the Hunchbacker crew to any infidel carries the punishment of a slow torturous death.'

Something cold tickled my spine. I glanced at the others and wondered if they hid their fear like me.

'What is their thing about slow torturous deaths?' Bit wanted to know.

'Maybe they've got a dungeon somewhere where they torture snitches on a rack or something,' guessed McKay. 'Or they might roast 'em like Joan of Arc.'

'It's all very childish,' said Venetia. 'Haven't they got anything better to do? G-Gore should be taking his zitty self to the nearest Superdrug.'

'Keep your heads down,' advised Boy from the Hills.

'Cos if they're willing to commit a slow torturous death to one of their own, what do you think they'll do to us?'

We all looked at each other and as one, slid down the mud bank a few centimetres.

'Ssssshhhhh!'

Kneeling beside the guy who was lying on the ground, G-Gore screamed into his ears. 'Do you swear on these commandments? Let me hear you, loud and clear! I implore you! DO YOU SWEAR?'

'Yes . . . yes, I swear,' came back the reply.

Saira opened her mouth. She was about to say something, but nothing came out. Venetia shook her head. Liccle Bit closed his eyes for a long second. I dropped a few more centimetres.

'Hold down his legs and arms,' ordered G-Gore.

Four guys stepped on to the bridge. Each held a limb of the bruv lying face down. It was gang ritual times ten, but I couldn't drag my eyes away.

'What the freak are they gonna do to him?' Bit wanted to know.

'I don't know,' replied Boy from the Hills. 'But I don't think it's gonna make him giggle. Little Mary won't be playing this game at her birthday party.'

'Who's little Mary when she's beating up her dolls?' I wondered.

'My spoilt cousin,' Boy from the Hills replied. 'She's six.'

'Lighters!' yelled G-Gore.

The rest of the Hunchbackers joined G-Gore on the

bridge. They took out their lighters from their pockets, formed a circle and clicked them on. They raised their arms. A yellow glow lit the still waters below.

'This is *sooo ridiculous and immature,*' said Venetia.

'But interesting,' replied Saira. 'We should film it. It might be . . . evidence.'

'*No!*' Boy from the Hills objected. 'That might lead to a world of trouble.'

'It's getting late and dark,' I added. 'This might go on all night. Let's dally before they scope us.'

'I wanna see what happens next,' insisted Bit.

'Me too.' McKay nodded.

'So do I,' added Saira.

Suddenly, G-Gore pulled out a long, curved knife from inside his coat. It had a serrated edge that glinted under the fire of the lighters.

'He's gonna delete him,' I said. 'Sign his autograph on his throat.'

'No, I don't think it's that,' replied Boy from the Hills.

G-Gore raised the knife to the heavens. Clouds had rolled by. A few stars appeared.

Then, G-Gore moved his blade across into the ring of fire. There, he roasted the sharp steel for a long minute.

'I think I know what's coming next,' said McKay. 'It's gonna sting big time.'

Venetia nodded. 'So do I . . . not good. Friggin ridiculous.'

'Yep.' Bit nodded. 'It's gonna hurt a liccle more than a Covid jab.'

225

'Be proud that you're marked with the letter H,' G-Gore said before he brought the tip of the knife to the boy's naked back. 'You're now a bona fide Hunchbacker. You carry the mark of the H.'

The Hunchbackers raised their fists into the air. 'H, H, H!' they chanted. 'H, H, H!'

'Aaaaaarrrrrgggghhh.'

I flinched and turned my head away. Venetia did the same, but the others couldn't avert their gazes.

I dared to watch again. The young Hunchbacker thrashed about in agony. His limbs were held tight. I could just about detect a ripple of smoke corkscrewing from the boy's back. It soon disappeared. G-Gore used a cloth to wipe something from the boy's shoulder.

I shook my head. 'I hope one of them has got a serious painkiller.'

'This is gross,' said Venetia. 'Maybe we should report this initiation ceremony shit to the feds?'

'Are you hazelnuts?' said McKay. 'The bruv will never spill to the feds. Didn't you hear the first commandment?'

G-Gore helped the boy to his feet. He looked about the same age as us, maybe even younger. G-Gore gave him a fist bump before offering him a bottle of drink. The new G tipped the liquid down his throat, and the rest of his crew raised their fists again. *'Hunchbackers will multiply. Hunchbackers will never die!'*

'I don't see any girls, so I don't know how they're gonna multiply,' chuckled Venetia.

'Ssssshhhhh,' warned Boy from the Hills. 'They're leaving.'

G-Gore placed a black beanie hat on the boy who'd just got carved. He then led them away through the woods.

'Hunchbackers will multiply. Hunchbackers will never die,' we heard until the chants faded.

Boy from the Hills checked his compass. 'They're heading north,' he said. 'Back to Notre Dame.'

'Shall we go to the bridge?' asked Saira.

'Let's wait a couple of minutes,' Boy from the Hills advised.

I counted the seconds down. I wasn't gonna lie, I wanted to jump on my Crongton bike and hot-wheel home. I didn't want to crash into G-Gore and let him Etch-A-Sketch a big H into my flesh . . . or worse.

'You guys go to the bridge,' Saira said after a good few minutes of silence. 'I'm gonna change into the wetsuit.'

We did as we were told.

20

Three Hundred Centimetres Beneath the Pond

There were dead leaves, green scum, crisp packets and a condom floating on the water. The odd twig too. I sniffed something toxic, but I couldn't guess what it was. Maybe a squashed frog.

I peered into the trees but couldn't spot any Hunchbackers. I breathed a little easier.

On the bridge itself, there were etchings and carvings in the woodwork.

BLADE JOHNSON, LOYAL HUNCHBACKER, WOZ 'ERE.

I read several more.

SMOKEY DAVIS, DEDICATED G-GORE SOLDIER.

Three Hundred Centimetres Beneath the Pond

'Maybe we should jack the bridge,' I laughed. 'Take it apart and burn it.'

'Burn everything with gangster graffiti on it,' said Venetia.

Saira joined us on the crossing. She had taken off her trainers and socks. She tucked her long hair under a swimming hat. The wetsuit showed off her toned body shape. 'Goggles?' she demanded.

Boy from the Hills gave her the specs. Saira polished them with her elbow. There was a dose of dread in her eyes.

'You can still change your mind,' said Boy from the Hills. 'I'll dive in if you want.'

'Yes.' Venetia nodded. 'This pond's not too clean. To be honest, it looks grimier than the boys' toilets at school.'

'That's more than disgusting,' agreed McKay.

'How do you know?' asked Juniper.

'Using my imagination,' replied Venetia.

Saira searched our eyes. 'I've not cycled all this way to mouse out of it now. Manjaro's treasure might be waiting for us down there. Or it might not be. I'm gonna find out, otherwise it'll bug the brain cells outta me.'

Before I could holler, 'Don't do it! It's not worth it,' Saira dived into the pond. The splash of water slapped our faces. She vanished under the surface.

'She friggin did it!' I said. 'She's in that toxic, slimy water!'

I leaned over the railings.

'I feel as if I need a shower just scoping the water,' said Venetia. 'Hope her one at home is working again.'

Boy from the Hills began to strip.

'What are you doing?' asked McKay.

'Getting ready in case she needs help,' replied Boy from the Hills.

'Give her a chance to have a look,' said Venetia. 'Her swimming is top-rated.'

Fifteen seconds later, Saira's head broke the surface. 'Can't see anything,' she said. 'It's too dark. It's about two or three metres deep. I have to feel with my hands.'

She gathered in a long breath and plunged in again. This time she was gone for more than half a minute. Boy from the Hills had pulled off his jacket and T-shirt. He was about to take off his trainers when Saira's head popped up again. 'I have to swim further along,' she said. 'Can't feel anything yet apart from sand and stones.'

'Saira,' Venetia called out. 'Don't bother!'

Before Venetia could protest any more, Saira disappeared once again. Something in the back of my mind told me that this could go wrong.

'Go and get her!' I urged Boy from the Hills. 'Tell her to come out.'

Boy from the Hills nodded. He was just about to jump in when Saira emerged from the polluted waters. She spat out pond grime. She took off the goggles, wiped her eyes and blinked furiously. Using one arm, she swam to a wooden post that supported the bridge. 'I've got something,' she said. 'Take it!'

She dragged a large rectangular object across the water.

At first, I couldn't make out what it was. It was covered in a brown-green goo, Sellotape and bubble wrap. Liccle Bit reached out for it and lifted it on to the bridge.

'There's another one down there,' said Saira. 'Give me two secs.'

Saira pulled on her goggles and plummeted again.

Time stilled.

We stared at each other for a long second. Words didn't need to be spoken. *Manjaro's treasure*. It was the biggest *oh my God* moment in all my days. We wiped away the gunk and ripped off the Sellotape and bubble wrap.

It was a black cabin case.

McKay lifted it above his head. He shook it. 'Frizzle my sizzles!' he exclaimed. 'There's something in it. Don't know what.'

'Then freaking open it!' urged Venetia.

Boy from the Hills zipped it open. The zip got snagged in a long weed. Boy from the Hills tugged at it. Out fell something wrapped in see-through plastic, like what they use for suits when they're dry-cleaned. Venetia was the first to tear the plastic open. Her eyes got big like a cute Disney cartoon character. 'Oh my friggin days!'

Liccle Bit's mouth wobbled. 'It's more,' he began. 'It's more . . . Frig my living paintbrushes.'

Bundles of ten-pound and twenty-pound notes bound in elastic bands. I had never seen so much money in all my life.

'How . . . how much do you think is there?' I asked.

'We're gonna need all the maths teachers at school to count it,' replied McKay.

'Give me a hand!' yelled Saira as she heaved another cabin case across the water.

I ran to assist her and pulled the luggage out of the pond.

Climbing on to the bridge, Saira stared at the wads of cash in the first cabin case. 'Shit is real! Oh my life! It's real! I just *knew* I wasn't wrong with Manjaro's riddle.'

'Kiss my knights!' McKay hollered at the heavens.

'I don't believe it!' said Bit. 'Just don't believe it! What are we gonna do with all of it?'

'Keep our promises,' replied Venetia. 'Gonna make a fat donation to the bereavement fund.'

'Sssssshhhhh,' warned Boy from the Hills. 'Remember, the Hunchbackers were here just a few minutes ago. Let's pack the money into our backpacks and roll outta here quick-time.'

As Saira pulled out a towel from her rucksack, we split the cash into our backpacks.

'It's all dry,' Venetia said. 'Dry like a Rich Tea biscuit left in the sun.'

After frantically tearing the bubble wrap and Sellotape off the second cabin case, I unzipped it. Wads of notes sealed in see-through plastic dropped out. As I grabbed the money and studied the water and foil marks, I closed my eyes for a long second and reopened them. I wanted to check if I was dreaming. 'Blazing sandpits!'

'Hurry up,' urged Boy from the Hills. His gaze flicked towards the trees.

'I'm gonna get out of this wetsuit before I start walking funny,' Saira said. 'It's tight around my shoulders and crotch.'

We worked quickly and efficiently.

I glanced at the heavens and made out a quarter moon. The stars twinkled brighter. Cool breezes licked the fingertips of the high branches. *Life can be exciting sometimes!*

'How much are we gonna put into your bereavement fund?' McKay asked Venetia.

'Dunno,' she replied. 'Most of it, I guess. Might use what's left over to take a shopping trip to the expensive ends of the Broadway.'

'Jonah,' Boy from the Hills called me. 'You can buy the name-brand spikes you want now. Money isn't an option. What did Usain Bolt wear? You're gonna mash up the school champs.'

'Don't bless my neck with the gold medal yet,' I replied. 'I still need to work on my stamina.'

Something caught Liccle Bit's eye. He stopped packing his backpack and slowly raised his head. He didn't like what he saw.

21

The Boy With the Yellow Teeth

Bit stood still and stared towards the trees. He then stepped off the bridge and squinted. I followed his direction of gaze.

Standing on his lonesome was the short boy who had presented the bell to G-Gore. He'd appeared from nowhere. I wondered how long he had stood there. He was no more than twelve. His eyes spoke of fear. Mud stained his left cheek. A raggedy black beanie hat covered his head. His black hair fell on to his shoulders. He wore a black puffa jacket and black jeans. Black Adidas trainers wrapped his toes.

'We . . .' Liccle Bit gently spoke to the boy. 'We weren't spying on your crew. We've just found something . . . something in the pond. It . . . it belongs to us.'

'Yeah,' Venetia said softly. 'Why we're here hasn't got anything to do with you or your crew. Trust me on that.'

The Boy With the Yellow Teeth

The boy took a pace back. Then another. He glanced over his shoulder. He wiped his lips. He stared at McKay then back to Bit. He sucked in a breath. His arms and fingers were stiff, as if he had stepped out of a freezer. I guessed he expected us to attack him.

My pulse banged my temples. My heart slammed my ribs. Something nibbled my guts. My toes itched to run. *Why am I so freaked out by a young kid? He might just keep his mouth sealed if we go polite on him.*

Bit held up his palms. 'We're not in any crew,' he said. 'I promise you that. We haven't come for any trouble.'

'We're not into any drama,' added Venetia. 'We're on a school field trip. That's all.'

What happened next seemed to take place in slow motion.

The boy's mouth opened. His teeth were wonky and yellow. His gums were black. Bit took a step towards him with his hands up in the air. The boy's eyes flicked from left to right. I sensed he wasn't alone.

I rammed whatever notes I had left in my hands into my backpack. Boy from the Hills did the same. McKay about-turned and fat-toed towards our hiding place. I had never seen him sprint so fast.

'SPIES!' the boy screamed. 'THERE'S ANOTHER GANG HERE! SPIES! SPIES!'

I swapped a rapid glance with Venetia before I set my gears and blazed back to our hiding place. 'Saira!' I called. 'Saira! Jump on your bike. Get outta here!'

McKay somersaulted over the mud bank, took a roll and mounted his bike. He left a trail of leaves in his wake. *Seriously impressive.*

Juniper and Venetia were as quick as each other, their arms and elbows chopping the air as they raced up the mud bank.

Before I made the leap, I glanced behind me.

Hunchbackers hunted us with serious intent from both sides of the pond. They looked proper ferocious.

'Wipe them off our lands!' G-Gore roared. '*Don't* let the infidel get away.'

'They're PDOs!' somebody else cried. 'Kill the PDOs!'

'Oh my sweet Jesus! They think we're the Poverty Driven Orphans,' I yelled. 'Oh my God!'

McKay was the first to hit the trail. Then Saira. Liccle Bit had problems placing his foot on the pedal – it kept slipping off. Boy from the Hills zoomed ahead while adjusting his backpack. Juniper cycled like mad, her green dungarees camouflaging her, and merged into the darkness. My backside didn't even touch the seat when I started pedalling. It was risky to accelerate along the zigzagging lane.

'*Shit!*'

I looked behind.

Venetia had fallen off her bike. She had hit something. Her front wheel was proper mangled. Her forehead creased in terror.

I braked and skidded to a stop, did an about-turn and raced to rescue her.

Liccle Bit reached Venetia before I could. 'Jump on!' he urged. 'Quick!'

Venetia thought about it. She looked at her broken bike, then back to Bit. 'Step it up!' he urged.

'Kill the PDO!' a Hunchbacker screamed in pursuit.

'Delete the infidel!'

Is this gonna be my last day?

A glint of something shiny caught my eye.

'Jump on the freaking bike and hold on tight!' Liccle Bit insisted.

Venetia did as she was told.

The Hunchbackers were only thirty metres away. The others had stopped ahead. Liccle Bit pumped his legs in a desperate effort to pick up speed.

Twenty metres away.

I cycled behind Liccle Bit, reached out my right hand to his saddle and pushed them along.

Fifteen metres away.

'Pedal, Bit! Pedal!'

Their bike rocked from right to left. Venetia's legs went up and down like a gone-wrong windmill. She wrapped her arms around Bit's waist. For one short second, I thought she was going to drop. I almost lost balance myself as I shoved them along.

'Pedal! Bit, pedal!'

I hadn't switched on my front light. I could only follow the red reflective lamps of the others ahead. We veered off the path.

Something was thrown at me. It smacked my rear wheel. I almost toppled over but just about kept my balance. I concentrated every energy I had into my thighs. *Pedal, Jonah, pedal!*

I didn't know what was gonna burst first: my heart, my lungs or my leg muscles. I was thankful for the extra stamina training that Mr Smallwood had offered. I remembered G-Gore's commandment about a slow torturous death.

Pedal, Jonah, pedal!

Ten seconds later, I dared to glance behind.

Shit!

By the way they were cursing us, I didn't think they thought of a slow torturous death. More like a rapid, stake-in-the-heart vampire one.

I cycled on ahead. 'Follow me,' I yelled.

I led them through woods, gullies, narrow lanes and sharp turns. We came to a clearing and I checked behind once more.

The Hunchbackers had given up the hunt.

Phew! Oh my life! Thank Jesus, Allah, Buddha, all the Hindu gods and Mr Smallwood.

We cycled like demons escaping judgement day all the way to the cross path. Ravenswood was now a looming shadow behind us. *Phew again.* Violent swear words faded on the breeze.

'That was too close,' I said. 'For one sec I thought I was gonna end up as Notre Dame food.'

'I thought . . .' Venetia started. 'I thought . . .'

She dropped her head and covered her face with her hands. Bit and Saira went to comfort her. 'Thank you,' she said to Bit. 'You saved my clumsy self.'

'You're worth it,' Bit replied.

'*No* more cadazy missions,' I said. 'They could've caught us, knocked us out with that bell and flung us into that grimy water!'

'It was proper slimy.' Saira nodded. 'But hey-de-ho! We got the Gs! And I mean a luggage-full of Gs. I am sooooo stepping to Crongton Broadway at the weekend.'

'We won't be stepping anywhere if we don't roll outta here quick-time,' warned Boy from the Hills. 'G-Gore looked proper pissed.'

'And he's gonna be desperate to give us a slow tortoise death,' I added.

'It could've been worse,' said Juniper.

'How?' I asked.

'We might've crashed into ghosts and duppies. We're lucky they're still sleeping.'

We laughed together and set off again towards the Ashburton Road. Bit and Venetia rode twenty metres behind us. They were in a deep convo. 'Keep up!' I hollered at them.

Bit simply smiled.

'Can't we rest for another two minutes?' asked McKay.

'*No*,' replied Boy from the Hills. 'Hunchbackers might still be about. They can jump on bikes too.'

'Now we know why peeps don't roam on Fireclaw Heath,' said Saira. 'It's where the Notre Dame crew hold their messed-up ceremonies.'

'Can't believe they carved that boy's back,' said Bit. 'Smoke came out of his flesh. That was traumatic.'

'Getting chased by them was stressful times ten,' I added. 'Can we roll outta here quick-time? I'm not gonna feel safe till my toes are kissing South Crong concrete.'

We pushed hard to the Ashburton Road and didn't stop until we reached the Crongton roundabout.

Sweet heavy traffic and peeps on pavements. Witnesses!

McKay was the first to dismount his bike. 'My legs are saying to my brain I'm gonna quit on you,' he said. 'And I'm peckish.'

McKay took out his corned-beef roll and shared the fairy cakes. 'Don't say I don't look after you,' he said. 'Remember this when we hit the Cheesecake Lounge. I'm not paying a diddly for my super-duper raspberry deluxe.'

'We can buy the whole menu,' Saira said. 'They've even got a VIP room where we can have a private party. Let's hire a DJ! Let's have a dance contest.'

'All good, all good,' said Boy from the Hills. 'But first, let's get back to McKay's and count this money.'

'Sssssshhhhh,' I warned. 'Don't want anyone to hear.'

'Your pops stepped to work today?' Venetia asked McKay.

'He sure has,' McKay replied. 'We'll be home alone. I might even have some envelopes to slap everyone's share of the money in.'

'Gonna need more than envelopes,' said Bit. 'Might need a treasure chest or two.'

'My shoeboxes might come into use.' McKay smiled.

'Crongton Broadway!' Saira raised her tones. 'I'll be seeing you! I wonder if I've still got that Louis Vuitton catalogue?'

'We'll look up some garms online,' promised Venetia.

22

Unexpected Guests

We returned our bikes to the stand behind Crongton Central bus station and made our way to McKay's slab.

We agreed that if anyone asked, we'd say the bike that Venetia used got jacked by Notre Dame kerb-bandits.

As usual, the lifts had gone wrong in McKay's block. 'Today of all days!' McKay moaned as we climbed the stairs.

'Are you sure my bike is safe downstairs chained up to the rail?' asked Boy from the Hills.

'Er . . . no,' McKay admitted. 'But if it gets jacked, you can now buy a new one.'

'What kind of spikes are you gonna buy?' Venetia asked me.

'The Puma Evospeed,' I replied. 'They have a suede lining and they're made specifically for Mondo-type tracks.'

'What's a Mondo-type track?' Juniper wanted to know.

Unexpected Guests

'Those tracks used for the World Championships and Olympics,' I explained.

We finally made it to the seventh floor. McKay puffed hard as he took his keys from his pocket. I blew out a breath of relief – I didn't feel too safe trodding the South Crong streets with wads of cash strapped to my back.

'You got any drink in your yard?' Venetia asked.

'Yeah,' McKay replied. 'Got some Ribena and government juice.'

'What's government juice?' Boy from the Hills wanted to know.

'Water,' replied Juniper.

McKay pushed his key into the lock. He clicked on the hallway light. We entered single file. There was another light switched on in the open-plan kitchen and living room.

Oh no! Serious blisters!

Three people sat around the kitchen table, empty mugs and phones on the table in front of them. They were all older than us and related to us. One of them was my sister, Heather. The other two were Bit's sis, Elaine, and McKay's older bruv, Nesta.

Everything paused.

Something weird cramped up my leg muscles. Then I think my heart stopped.

Half of me hoped that Heather hadn't scoped me. Every urge in my bones told me to about-turn and zoom all the way home. I even looked out of the window as a possible escape route.

I glanced at McKay, and something strange was happening to his face. I couldn't work out if he was happy to see his bruv after the longest time, or terrified.

Juniper was the only one who moved. 'I need a drink,' she said. 'Gonna pour me some government juice.'

Elaine stood up first. Her eyes blazed like gas rings. She placed her fists on her hips. Liccle Bit looked as if he needed one of those things that doctors used to reboot peeps' hearts.

'You guys have been stepping on enemy kerbs, haven't you?' she hollered at Bit. 'Don't even think about denying it or I'll slap you down to the ground floor. What's wrong with you? You go roaming in North Crong and Fireclaw Heath? Are you freaking insane? Don't you know what's going on with this North Crong–South Crong war?'

Elaine rushed up to Bit and pressed a hard finger into his forehead. I was well glad that Heather wasn't so fierce. 'What did I friggin tell you?' Elaine yelled. 'Come on, Mr Big Man, what did I tell you?'

Spittle flew out of Elaine's mouth. Bit mopped his forehead and stared at the floor.

'To ... to keep out of dangerous ends,' Bit replied. 'And keep my ass outta any dangerous situation.'

'Yes!' Elaine yelled. 'Yes! I did! To keep your short ass outta drama and strife! And what do you go and do? Eh? Eh? Your bones just about escaped the last time you went up to alien ends. And now this?'

Unexpected Guests

'Stop shouting up the place,' said Nesta. 'I might've done the same ting at their age. It's an exciting mission. How could young pups resist it? Manjaro proper teased them.'

Nesta walked up to McKay and offered him a long glare. 'I'm glad to see you breathing, but you should've leaked this mission to me before you stepped into enemy ends.'

'Sorry,' McKay managed. 'But you've been missing for a long stretch. It's . . . it's good to see you though, bro.'

'Good to see you too,' Nesta replied. 'But it seems as if every time I bust back into your life, you're doing some dumb shit and I have to sort it out.'

'Dumb shit?' McKay repeated. 'We found untold grands!'

'Hold up a minute,' Boy from the Hills said to Nesta. He narrowed his eyes. 'How did you know about the mission?'

Nesta, Elaine and Heather swapped glances. Juniper didn't even bother to look for a cup – she drank straight from the cold tap. McKay tipped Ribena into a jug. He took out seven glasses from a cupboard.

I *sooooo* needed a drink.

'Sit down,' ordered Nesta.

Apart from McKay, we all parked ourselves on the sofa and the armchair.

'Elaine visited someone today,' revealed Heather.

'Who?' I asked.

'Manjaro,' Heather replied.

Silence.

Every time his name was mentioned, this toxic menace polluted the air.

'He wanted to see Jerome,' Elaine explained. 'Trust me, I hate what that man's done but he had a right to see his son.'

McKay served the drinks. I side-eyed Heather and she glared back at me. I knew she was gonna give me her full range of cussing when I reached home. I just hoped she wouldn't snitch to Mum and Pops.

'And after he saw Jerome and played with him,' Elaine resumed, 'he told me about this *liccle game* and the treasure trail. He said he wanted to teach a liccle history to the youth of South Crong.'

'What a grass!' Juniper said. 'He spilled about the whole mission? And he's meant to be the king G of these ends? Can't trust anyone these days.'

Elaine nodded. 'He leaked like a tea bag. It's a game for him. He cracked up laughing. He said it was a good way for you to learn shit that they don't teach in schools.'

'He wasn't wrong,' said Saira. 'I for one learned about Marcus Garvey and the Irish nationalists.'

'He thought you guys would never go for it,' Elaine continued. 'He half expected that when he'd served his time, he could go back for it.'

'At first, we couldn't believe it,' said Heather. She stared at me and held my gaze for a long three seconds. 'Then I called Nesta, and Nesta dinged the Lady to find out if it was true.'

'Lady P!' I guessed.

'Yes!' Heather nodded. 'She told me how you'd stepped

into a car to Manjaro's hideout, and how he'd given you a choice.'

'Pinchers kidnapped me,' I protested.

Nesta looked at me hard. 'Pinchers' name doesn't escape this room,' he said. 'The feds are still investigating his deletion. Don't spill Lady P's name either. Does that register with you guys?'

I nodded. Saira sank the rest of her drink. Liccle Bit dropped his head and Juniper read a message on her phone. Boy from the Hills gazed at the blank TV.

'I said, *does* that register with *you* guys?' Nesta raised his voice.

'YEAH, YEAH, YEAH!' We all nodded.

'You know Lady P?' Venetia asked Nesta.

'Ask no question and I can't tell you no lie,' replied Nesta.

'Which one of you dived into the pond?' Elaine wanted to know.

Saira stood up. 'Me,' she said. 'And before you start stomping on my bruvs, we went on this mission cos we didn't want any Gs to find that money. We planned to do something good with it.'

'Yeah.' Venetia nodded. 'We were gonna put most of it into the bereavement fund for families who have lost folks in the South–North Crong war. That's the pretty truth.'

Elaine, Nesta and Heather traded glances again.

'I've heard about that support group,' Heather said. 'I can't lie. It's a good cause.'

'They're not messing,' added McKay as he sank his drink. 'Just trying to do some good in the parish.'

'And nice up your pockets?' suggested Elaine.

'You wanna give us a smackdown cos of that?' Bit asked.

'*No,*' Elaine replied. 'We . . . we just want you to be safe. There's a lot of shit going down that you guys don't know about.'

'We stepped into the heart of darkness in North Crong,' Juniper said. 'And no one troubled us.'

'The librarian wasn't playing,' I added. 'Wouldn't like to think what he would've done if he'd caught me.'

'He was the only speed bump in the road,' Venetia said. 'And the Hunchbackers on Fireclaw Heath. We wasn't expecting that.'

'You're playing with your lives!' Elaine shouted. 'This isn't a game. Peeps your age have been merked. In the last two years I've attended three funerals.'

Silence.

I stared at the fridge.

I willed someone to speak.

'What's done is done,' said Nesta finally. 'Just don't set off on any cadazy missions in the future.'

'We won't,' I said and hesitated before asking, 'You're not gonna spill to our parents, are you?'

Nesta thought about it. He turned to Elaine and Heather. My sis glanced at me as if she was considering some kinda medieval punishment.

'No,' Elaine said. 'But if I even sniff that you're out of the

Unexpected Guests

ends again on another dangerous mission, I'll leak to the feds, the FBI, MI5 *and* all your parents.'

'That's a relief,' said Venetia.

'Let's see the money,' ordered Nesta. 'Where is it? I know you found it cos of the grin on my bruv's face when you rolled in. Is it in your rucksacks?'

We opened our backpacks and emptied the wads of cash on to the kitchen table. A few bundles dropped on the floor. Boy from the Hills picked them up.

'How much money did Manjaro leave on his treasure trail?' asked Nesta.

'Altogether,' replied Elaine, 'forty grand. It was the same amount he wanted to give to me.'

Forty grand! Smoking starter guns!

I tried to divide forty into seven, but I guessed Heather would tell me a big fat no if I asked for my share of the booty.

Nesta turned to Elaine. 'We'll have to launder this,' he said. 'And be careful about it.'

'What . . . what do you mean, "launder"?' asked Venetia. 'We stepped into dangerous zones. We found the money. Don't we get a say?'

'What we mean is,' Heather explained, 'we can't just spend this money in the shops or take it to the bank. For one thing, the notes might be hot, and for another, peeps are gonna get proper suspicious if you're paying for shit with nuff bunches of notes. Word gets around.'

'Then what?' Juniper wondered. 'It'll be a waste if we

can only use it for a game of Monopoly.'

'Lady P will have to deal with it,' Elaine said. 'She's got the links. We can trust her.'

'Rewind, rewind,' said Venetia. 'Don't we get a slice?'

'My liccle bruv might get a slap on his forehead.' Elaine raised her voice again. 'His reward is me not smacking the eyebrows off his forehead.'

'But we followed the treasure hunt!' protested Saira. 'We solved the riddles, stepped into North Crong Library and I dived into the toxic pond on Fireclaw Heath. *Don't* tell me I did that all for sweet diddly zero?'

McKay stepped up to Nesta. He stared at him the way brothers do. 'Let's be real, Nesta,' he said. 'You can never plant a toe on North Crong ends. You would've never made it to North Crong Library. You're their public enemy numero uno. Everyone knows that.'

Nesta bit his top lip.

It suddenly slapped my brain cells. Nesta might be the one Lady P was referring to when she said somebody had to step up. *Oh my Knights. I wonder if McKay's on this page?*

'We deserve a slice!' Juniper said.

Heather glared at me. I decided to rest my tongue.

'Fifteen grand for the youth club building fund and fifteen for the bereavement charity,' offered Elaine. 'And remember, that money was meant for my son, Jerome. But I can't take it.'

'Why not?' Venetia wanted to know.

'Manjaro got the money from peeps in our ends,' Elaine

Unexpected Guests

explained. 'A sweet portion of it from bruvs and sisters who got hooked on dragon-hip pills. Too many lives have been lost for that shit. Most of it should go back into the community. It's the right thing to do.'

'What about the rest?' Bit wanted to know.

Nesta searched our eyes. 'Five hundred each. For working out the riddles, stepping to North Crong and finding the money in that toxic pond.'

'Five hundred!' Venetia repeated. 'Liberties! We came within seconds of being deleted by G-Gore and his crew. Nah, man. That's not gonna compute . . . eight hundred!'

Venetia stood up. She took a step towards Nesta. 'I'm not taking anything less than eight hundred.'

I cautiously nodded.

Nesta gazed at Heather and Elaine. They communicated something with their eyes.

'Eight hundred it is,' said Nesta. 'But if I hear that you guys are stepping into foreign zones again, I'll take the eight hundred back and spill to the North Crong on every move you make.'

Heather side-eyed me. 'You can spend some of your share on those new spikes you're always going on about. The rest can go towards next month's rent.'

I couldn't kill the grin spreading from my lips.

'What about the other five thousand two hundred?' Saira asked.

'That'll be Lady P's cut for laundering the money,' Elaine replied. 'And other . . . administration costs.'

'That'll keep her in neat earrings,' I said.

'Do we have a deal?' Nesta asked. He searched our eyes.

'Deal,' Venetia agreed.

'Right,' Nesta said. 'If everyone can excuse me, I wanna do some catching up with my young bro.'

'Of course,' Heather replied. She gave me a brutal side-eye. 'And *I've* got some career advice for my younger bruv.'

23

Usain Bolting for Glory

Three weeks later, Heather was still offering career advice. I had to tolerate it. At least she didn't leak my part in the hunt for Manjaro's treasure to my parents.

'Don't even think about landing your toes on any badlands,' she said to me over the breakfast table. 'If you do, I'll tie rocks to your ankles and fling you in that toxic pond on Fireclaw Heath myself.'

Outside school, I didn't see too much of my friends cos I stepped up my training with Mr Smallwood.

For one of our conditioning and stamina sessions, Mr Smallwood led us to Falcon Ridge.

I sided up to Merlene Quarrie. 'What's up?' I greeted.

'All good,' she said. 'Feel as if I'm ready for the champs.'

'Can . . . can I ask you a personal question?'

'Depends how personal,' Merlene replied.

'Er . . . are you single?'

Merlene smiled. 'Are you hitting on me, Jonah?'

'No, no, no,' I quickly replied. 'Just . . . asking.'

'It's just that I don't date guys,' Merlene confirmed.

'So . . . that means . . . you know. Er . . .'

'Yes, Jonah. Shock horror. I like girls. Don't you?'

'Oh, er, um . . . yes I do . . . That's cool.'

'To answer your question,' Merlene added. 'I'm single.'

Hours later, I leaked this news to Saira. The smile on Saira's face was wide enough to span the pond on Fireclaw Heath.

Heather kept her promise and bought me my Puma spikes. With the rest of my slice from Manjaro's treasure, she paid towards the rent. I didn't ask how Lady P had laundered the money or how she'd placed the cash in Heather's account. She made me promise that I'd never leak Lady P's name again or Manjaro's treasure.

'It's a new start for us,' Heather said. 'It won't be easy with Dad not being here, but we'll get through it. The ups and downs of life. Now, make sure you win the school champs or otherwise I'll drag you to G-Gore!'

My family and friends were all in the stand as I settled my feet in the starting blocks for the school regional championships four-hundred-metre final. I had won my semi-final. The sun blessed the afternoon, and there was only a slight headwind in the back straight. I looked down at my Puma spikes. I was drawn in lane three at the Monks

Orchard athletic track.

I glanced into the stand again. Venetia, Juniper and Saira held a banner that Liccle Bit had designed. It showed an image of me blazing around the Crongton Heath track. *Rapid Jonah Hani! Faster than a peckish cheetah, quicker than Maverick in a Top Gunner!*

I didn't want to let them down.

Mum and Pops were there. Heather stood between them. Mr Smallwood, standing with arms crossed in a grey baggy tracksuit, looked on intensely from near the long jump pit.

The starter climbed his three steps to the podium. He wore beige trousers and a blue blazer. His starter gun had a short barrel. I felt the pulse of my heartbeat in my throat.

'On your marks . . . get set!'

Bang.

I half stumbled out of my blocks. Smallwood had told me to take it easy around the first bend. *'Keep your body relaxed,'* he'd instructed.

I might have been too casual, because as I raced into the back stretch, I was in last place.

I gradually increased my speed. I caught up with the guy in lane four. I gained confidence as his form began to unravel. I heard the shouts and roars from the crowd.

I reached the last bend. I guessed I was in fourth place. The runners in lanes six and seven were in front. Mr Smallwood had told me to never look over my shoulder, but I sensed somebody on my inside was ahead of me.

The finish straight was ahead. My thigh muscles screamed. My calves were sore. I had little left.

'Come on, Jonah!' someone screamed.

I pinned my head back. I swallowed in a mouthful of air. I closed my eyes for half a second. I imagined the Hunchbackers chasing me. Beanie hats and long blades. The letter H carved on their naked backs. A whole range of cursing.

I found something.

I ran scared.

'Jonah! You can do it!'

I glanced to my right. In lane six, one athlete was half a metre ahead of me. I checked to my left. Another runner was two metres clear.

A final push.

'Jonah! Blaze along that freaking track!'

I was sure that was Saira's voice.

I gave it one final effort.

My stride shortened.

Lactic acid killed my speed.

My lung power was about to burst.

My rival in lane six must've suffered worse.

I inched ahead of him.

The finishing line was close.

Ten metres away.

I did something that Mr Smallwood always advised against.

I lunged for the line instead of racing through it. I had to correct myself to stop falling over.

I crossed in second place. I looked for Mum in the stands. She politely applauded while my pops jumped up and down as if a snake had wriggled up his trousers. My Crongton Knights went totally nuclear. Juniper did a strange dance.

Second in the regional champs! Second! If I do some hard training I could get to the Olympics.

Mr Smallwood ran up to me and lifted me on to his shoulder. 'You see!' he said. 'All that stamina training came into use. Next year, make sure you win!'

The applause of the crowd made me feel tingly. It had been an age since I'd seen Mum and Pops so happy. It felt good.

Smallwood placed me down, but my head was still in the sky. 'Got a message from your sister, Heather,' he said. 'She's gonna take you and your mates to the Cheesecake Lounge to celebrate. Congratulations, Jonah. You deserve it.'

I waved at my friends before I left the track. I felt ten feet tall as I stepped beneath the stand and headed to the showers.

Fifteen minutes later, I emerged from the changing rooms. Juniper was waiting for me.

'What is it?' I asked. 'Aren't we going to the Cheesecake Lounge? Are my parents still here?'

'Your pops drove your mum home,' she said. 'Are they getting back together?'

I would've loved to have answered yes. The brutal truth told me it was highly unlikely. As Heather said, it was the ups and downs of family life. At least I had two parents who loved me. Others were not so blessed.

'Don't think so,' I finally replied. 'They're just supporting me. What are you doing down here?'

Juniper looked to her right, and then her left. She lowered her voice. 'I wanted to tell you something before we meet up with your sis.'

'Tell me what?' I wondered.

'Something has happened,' she said. 'We have to go on another mission. It's a life-and-death ting. Can't spill to anyone about it.'

'You're joking.'

'Am I?'

'Juniper! Don't mess with me!'

She flashed me a smile.

I could never tell if she was playing or being serious.

'Don't tell me anything,' I said. 'I just want to sample a super-duper raspberry deluxe cheesecake.'

'Just joking,' she laughed. 'Just wanna say you made us all proud today, no messing.'

'Really?' I asked.

'Yeah.' She nodded. 'Peeps who live in South Crong have to deal with a binful of shit. You know – family break ups and all that drama you've just been through. For me, it's all about the shoplifters who I sometimes sit in class with and friends of my pops begging for credit.

I can't tell you how much that stresses us out.'

'That must be hard.' I nodded.

'It is,' Juniper agreed. 'Then there's the North and South Crong wars that'll probably go on till I'm a cranky grandma. And worse of all, the colour of the school uniform they ask us to wear. It's child abuse.'

I could do nothing but laugh.

'But you gave us something to shout for today,' Juniper continued. 'An event we looked forward to and were excited about. Big respect due!'

'Thanks.' I grinned.

'Now get your ass in fifth gear so we can make steps to the Cheesecake Lounge.' She raised her voice. 'I'm seriously peckish and you took so damn long!'

Alex Wheatle is the author of several acclaimed novels, many of them inspired by experiences from his childhood. He was born in Brixton to Jamaican parents and spent most of his childhood in a Surrey children's home. After a short stint in prison following the Brixton uprising of 1981, he wrote poems and lyrics and became known as the Brixtonbard. Alex has been shortlisted for numerous awards, including the Carnegie Medal and the YA Book Prize. He won the Guardian Children's Fiction Prize and was awarded an MBE for services to literature in 2008.

You can find out more about Alex here:

www.alexwheatle.com

Twitter: @brixtonbard

WELCOME TO CRONGTON, WHERE YOUR LOYALTY AND WITS WILL BE TESTED . . .

COLLECT THEM ALL.

'GRIPPING'
MALORIE BLACKMAN

'... ENRICHING AND LIFE-AFFIRMING'
INDEPENDENT

'... POWERFUL WRITING BY AN AUTHOR WITH GREAT TALENT AND GREAT HEART'
DAVID ALMOND

'A MAJOR VOICE IN BRITISH CHILDREN'S LITERATURE'
S. F. SAID

ALSO BY ALEX WHEATLE

'STUDDED WITH WHEATLE'S CHARACTERISTIC SLANG, NAOMI'S STORY IS BOTH HEARTBREAKING AND HILARIOUS, OFFERING NO EASY HAPPY ENDINGS, BUT A FLICKERING SENSE OF HOPE.'

GUARDIAN